IRISH GHOST STORIES

IRISH GHOST STORIES

PADRAIC O'FARRELL

Gill & Macmillan

Gill & Macmillan
Hume Avenue, Park West
Dublin 12
www.gillmacmillanbooks.ie
© *The Estate of the late Padraic O'Farrell 2004*
978 07171 3633 9
Original text design by
Identikit Design Consultants, Dublin
Illustrations by Kate Shannon
Print origination by Carole Lynch
Printed by CPI Group (UK) Ltd, Croydon, CRO 4YY

This book is typeset in 10/15 pt Adobe Garamond.

The paper used in this book comes from the wood pulp
of managed forests. For every tree felled, at least one tree
is planted, thereby renewing natural resources.

*A CIP catalogue record for this book is available
from the British Library.*

11 10 12

TO THE MEMORY OF
RELATIVES AND FRIENDS
WHO HAVE PASSED AWAY

PUBLISHER'S NOTE

Padraic O'Farrell died suddenly while this book was in preparation. He was, in the most literal sense, an officer and a gentleman. He had served with distinction as a colonel in the Irish army. His love of literature and drama was a constant in his life. On his retirement, he was able to dedicate himself fully to these pursuits. He was a prolific and punctilious author and a delightful companion. He died shortly after reading and approving the proofs of this book. He left everything just so, in good order, and is much missed.

CONTENTS

Introduction   11

1. The Green Lady of St Stephen's Green   15

2. Eyewitness Accounts   19

3. A Tragic Wedding Day   32

4. The Returning Friar   36

5. The *Great Eastern*   41

6. Nelly of the Glen   45

7. At Arm's Length   50

8. Curse of the Cassidys   53

9. Collier's '*Weakly*' Guest   55

10. The 'Ghost Room' at Maynooth   57

11. Personal Touch   61

12. Brief Encounters   65

13. Letter in a Library   80

14. The Kerry Dances   82

15. The Devil's Kitchen above Killakee   84

16. Lady of the Lake   90

17. The Devil and the Daughter of
     Loftus Hall   94

18. The Killing Kildares   98

19. Spike Island's Gaunt Gunner   102

20. Ghost Family Festival   105

21. Mistress and Servants   111

22. The Man in the Yellow House   119

23. The Heart's a Wonder   124

24. The Mayo Béicheadán   131

25. Bloody Sunday Revisited?   136

26. A Longford Dog   140

Glossary   143

INTRODUCTION

The ghost story genre merits a two-page, highlighted spread in *The Oxford Companion to English Literature* (ed. Margaret Drabble, 6th edition, 2000). In Ireland the genre has a special place because it provided the raw material for evenings of storytelling that were a common feature of country life up to the 1950s (and frequently beyond).

In December 2001 the deputy Lord Mayor of Cork, Councillor Mary Shields, opened the first ever All-Ireland Ghost Convention in Cork City Jail. Inspiration for the event had come from Richard T. Cooke, a psychotherapist and hypnotherapist. The *Cork Evening Echo* reported the event:

Unexplained psychic phenomenon fascinates and intrigues people from all walks of life. However, many are afraid, ashamed and embarrassed to come forward for fear of not being taken seriously and it is for this reason that [the] convention was established – to allow people to explore this fascinating area. Richard's theory on the existence or otherwise of ghosts is pragmatic. He says 'They operate on a different plane to us and don't conform to the normal rules that we understand, so you can't get specific proof to say, "yes they do" or "no they don't" exist. … It's more of a feeling people have and if they experience something, someone who is with them at the time might not. That doesn't mean what they experience wasn't real.'

Some of Cooke's accounts are included in the 'Ghost Family Festival' chapter in this book. Along with his colleague at Irish Millennium Publications, Catherine M. Courtney, and author Pauline Jackson, he has kindly allowed me to retell stories from their excellent book, *Ghosts of Cork*.

Celebrated people, as well as ordinary folk, have had strange experiences, and included here are those of the actor Mícheál Mac Liammóir and of playwright and author Hugh Leonard. In the *Evening Echo* on Saturday, 1 December 2001 the Lord of the Dance, Michael Flatley, acknowledged the presence of a ghost named Isabella in his Castlehyde home near Fermoy, County Cork. Oliver St John Gogarty claimed that he believed in ghosts but qualified his statement: 'I know that there are times, given the place which is capable of suggesting a phantasy, when those who are sufficiently impressionable may perceive a dream projected as if external to the dreamy mind: a waking dream due both to the dreamer and the spot.' (*As I was Going Down Sackville Street*, Dublin,1937)

There are many well-known Irish ghost stories and I tell some of them in this book. I have, however, leaned heavily on the side of less well-known tales; most of them previously unpublished. All the time, I claim the storyteller's privilege of using his own style and embellishments. If my accounts appear a little flippant occasionally, this does not imply that I have taken people's accounts less seriously than I should. I'm sure ghosts have a sense of humour too! To avoid repetition, I offer many of the stories without qualification as to their authenticity.

Many people have given me assistance in collecting these stories and I wish to thank them most sincerely. They include the librarians and staffs of the National Library of Ireland and of the County Libraries of Cork, Kildare, Leitrim, Westmeath and Wexford. I thank also the Topic Newspaper Group, Tim Cadogan, Richard T. Cooke, Catherine M. Courtney, Pauline Jackson, Vincent Kelly of Cork's *Evening Echo*, Jack Keyes Byrne, Ivor Young of Horetown Equestrian Centre, County Wexford, Comdt Victor Laing, Army Archives, Comdts Kevin Croke, Arthur Armstrong and Paul Buckley, Yvonne Croke, J.H.R Lindsay, Mary O'Malley of Maynooth College Visitors' Centre, Alice and Kevin Downes, Anne Waters, Hook Heritage Limited, Brendan O'Connor and Joan Daly.

The work of previous chroniclers of the paranormal must be acknowledged. These include: Jonah Barrington, Patrick Byrne, the Countess of Fingall, Sean Henry, Mr and Mrs S.C. Hall, Shane Leslie, Seumas MacManus, James Reynolds, John Sheehan, Lady Wilde, and my parents and neighbours in Staplestown, County Kildare, who told ghost stories to me over three score years ago.

As usual, my daughters Niamh and Aisling assisted with word-processing and my wife Maureen proofread for tricks played by gremlins, ghouls and things that go bump in the computer. Thanks again too to Fergal Tobin of Gill & Macmillan for his continuing encouragement, courtesy and friendship and to a gracious lady whose patience and politeness are exemplary, editor Deirdre Rennison Kunz.

Padraic O'Farrell, 2003

ONE

THE GREEN LADY OF ST STEPHEN'S GREEN

The Green Lady of St Stephen's Green, Dublin, features in a sad story of marital disharmony. A beautiful young woman became madly jealous of her husband and watched his every move suspiciously. She nagged him constantly until eventually they separated. The young mother lived 'on the Green' with her children, David and Isa. Perhaps because the boy had all the features of her estranged husband, his mother maligned him. His sister, however, received her adoration and enjoyed every attention.

David took to closeting himself in a large empty room upstairs. His health failed and he became morose. Isa came upon him unexpectedly one day and was amazed to find him happy and cheerful – almost looking healthy. He told her that he had seen a beautiful lady dressed in green, who had seemed about to join in his game of skittles when Isa interrupted.

'She is tall, with deep blue eyes and her skin is as fair as a lily. Her gorgeous red hair falls in ringlets down her back,' he said.

David's joy was short-lived. The same evening his mother summoned him to the drawing room to meet a big, stern-looking man.

'He is going to be your stepfather, David, and you will address him as "sir",' she said.

David became more miserable than ever and when the wedding took place and the man was permanently ensconced in their home, he began treating David even more harshly than his mother had done. The boy's health deteriorated as rapidly as did his spirits. He was feeling so utterly dejected that he did not wish to live any longer.

Late one night Isa was in bed when she heard voices in the top room. She got out of bed, put on her slippers and crept upstairs. She listened at the door of the room and heard David say, 'Oh, that would be so nice. Thank you very much.'

Isa opened the door and saw her brother in his nightshirt, sitting on the floor.

'Why are you not in your bedroom? You should be asleep by now. Mama will be furious if she finds you here,' she said.

'Oh, you awful thing, you frightened her away,' David replied crossly.

'Talking to your silly Green Lady, I suppose?' Isa sneered.

'Yes, and she told me the most wonderful thing. She says she is going to take me to a place where I will be always happy,' David smiled.

Isa scolded him, saying he was stupid. She told him to get back to his bedroom or she would inform their mother. David obeyed and soon they were both asleep in their own rooms.

As the city bells were tolling midnight, Isa awoke. Above their peals, she could hear a woman's most beautiful voice singing a strange air. She thought of David's story and went to see if he had gone back upstairs. She checked his room but he was sleeping soundly. She was just about to return to her room when the singing began again. Then her mother and stepfather came from their room and servants gathered at the bottom of the stairs, all looking frightened.

'Sure as God, it's the Banshee,' one of them whispered.

After a while, the singing stopped and they all returned to their rooms.

When Isa came down to her breakfast, the cook was standing outside the kitchen, idly cleaning a basin but looking anxiously upstairs.

'That's three anyway, thank heavens,' she said, 'but your brother is usually first down.'

Isa went into the dining room where her mother and stepfather were talking about the stupidity of people who believed in ghosts and Banshees and the like.

'Is your brother not with you? Go get him this instant,' her mother ordered.

Isa went to David's room but he was not in bed. She went to the deserted room upstairs but he was not there either. She rushed back and told everybody and a search of the house and its out-offices began. There was no sign of the lad.

Then the gardener spoke up. 'Did youse try the ladder that leads to the attic where the water tank is?'

'What would he be doing going up there?' the stepfather asked sceptically.

'You'd never know, sir.'

'Well, you go and look so.'

The gardener went up and returned with the dripping body of the boy in his arms. 'Drowned in the tank,' he murmured to the horrified gathering.

'I knew it was the Banshee we heard,' the cook wailed.

'No, it was his Green Lady,' Isa whispered.

TWO

EYEWITNESS ACCOUNTS

First-hand accounts of ghosts are rare but a farmer-poet from Cloghan, County Westmeath, wrote of his own experiences in the *Westmeath Topic* during 1978. John Sheehy's home was close to Killynon House. It had belonged to the Reynell family for close on five hundred years. The mansion no longer stands but John remembered well the large dwelling house occupied by the last surviving member of the Reynells, a bachelor and 'a cultured and benevolent character of Oxford standard'. His only sister kept house and supervised a retinue of servants. They often entertained other aristocratic friends and hosted meets of the Westmeath Hunt.

John's interests included water- and metal-divining, at which he was adept. He wrote short stories and poetry and loved the countryside and its ways and lore. He had often heard about horses, riders and hounds of centuries past galloping over Killynon estate in the dead of night and of neighbours hearing the sound of the hunting horn, the thunder of hooves and the 'Tally-ho!' of the eager ghostly followers. Local tradition stated that when there was a death in the Reynell family, the ancestors of the deceased gathered in the house and in its basement and later spilled out into the grounds. People of Cloghan heard their chattering and, sometimes, their carousing.

A large black dog cropped up in many tales. It even interfered in the amorous adventures of the staff. On one occasion a maid arranged to meet a local labourer at a small building by the tennis court. Neither could make any advances because the dog constantly circled round them. John did not take the stories very seriously – until he began noticing some very peculiar occurrences in and around Killynon House.

Late one autumn night, John was at the mearing of the Killynon property, looking for one of his beasts which had rambled from his haggard. He saw an orange glow moving through the estate about eight feet above the ground. It would stop for a while, then move on again. Too large for a will-o'-the-wisp, John nevertheless concluded that it was some similar phosphorescent light caused by combustion of methane. Then his heart gave a leap. Almost beside him was another man watching the light. This giant figure was standing by a stile leading into the estate. John did not know any neighbour who came close to the man's height. But he remembered a story he had heard years before about a dying member of the Reynell family calling a trusted herdsman to his bedside. He had promised, 'When I have left, you keep a close watch on the animals by day and I will keep vigil by night.' John wondered if he had stumbled upon the ghost of Reynell keeping his promise.

John was more amazed another evening when he was passing close to the house and heard 'the echo of many voices coming from the horse stalls'. He assumed there was a party going on – something that occurred frequently during the shooting season. He enquired the next day but was assured by the staff that not only was there no celebration the night before but the family members were all away and had given most of the servants a holiday. Soon afterwards, John noted that a close relative of the family died.

While in the house itself one day, John saw a young girl standing by the sink in the basement scullery. Her hands were resting on the sink and she remained rigid when he was passing by. He walked along the flags in the passage, stopped and looked back but the girl did not leave the scullery. Later John was sitting in the servants' dining hall and the housekeeper came to greet him. John asked her if they had hired extra staff. When she said they had not, he told her about the girl in the basement. They went to the scullery together but it was empty. It had no window and John had been watching its doorway all the time.

One of John's visits to the house brought him in view of the lawn and the avenue leading to the front door. It was a spring afternoon and he was dressed in heavy clothes to protect himself from a biting easterly wind. An old lady in a light blue, summery dress was walking along a gravel path that led to a large arched iron gate. He wondered why, at her age, she had no headgear and was not wrapped up warmly. Her route took her out of his sight for the two minutes it took him to reach a wicket gate leading to the back yard. When he approached the gate, however, she was nowhere to be seen. Then he remembered. Her features were those of a family member who had died a decade earlier!

About six months later the same garden was the setting for another of John's experiences. His potatoes had been blighted and he was visiting the garden hoping to buy some from the gardener. This was a man of few words and all of them blunt. He was working near the potting shed in the centre of the walled garden.

'The potatoes are a lot worse here,' he said, and pointing further down the garden, he added, 'You might find an odd good one down there if you are not too lazy to use a spade.'

John went to the place indicated and found the condition of the potatoes almost as bad as his own – only about one in thirty was free from blight. A deafening bang interrupted his work. The potting shed! All the terracotta pots must have fallen, he thought. He looked back at the gardener, who called for John to go into the shed with him. They went in and saw that nothing was broken. The gardener remarked that it was not the first time he had heard the noise. He said little more, despite John's attempts to make conversation, joking that he needed 'to keep a drop of holy water in the shed'.

John then went back to the drills, put the few good potatoes into a leather satchel, paid the gardener and left. As he was passing a large oak tree beside the path where he had seen the lightly clad lady previously, he heard a sharp crack, which he described as being like the smack of a golf ball being hit.

'It started at ground level,' he recalled, 'and moved upwards … into the boughs of the tree, crossing from one to the other. Then I found myself being pelted on the head and shoulders with large lumps of broken potatoes.'

Children playing a prank? Not possible. They could not have hidden in the branches, there was not enough cover. Someone flinging them from the garden? No. Much too great a distance. So John returned to the gardener with two handfuls of the broken potatoes. The man identified them as being from the garden but when he heard what had happened, he became pale and passed no further comment. John too lost a bit of colour when he returned to his satchel. It was where he had left it, but there was no trace of the other scraps of potato.

The last member of the family to occupy Killynon House was Richard Reynell. Before he left, he told John that he had seen apparitions but they did not worry him. He said that his dead aunt often came back to visit him.

When the estate changed hands, its new owner rented the house to a tenant who did not stay long. Nor did the next. A later occupant gave John permission to take a few laurel plants to make a hedge. He was bringing them home, tied in a bundle and slung over his shoulder about an hour before noon one bright morning. Moving through a grove, he felt his load swinging from side to side and thought a briar might have caught it. He stopped to check but could see nothing that might have caused the movement. Off he went again and this time his shoulders began jerking as the load began moving up and down, 'as if some unseen hand was tugging at the laurels'. Then the same force hoisted the bundle about three feet into the air with such strength that the rope slapped against John's face and knocked his hat off.

Rather than feeling frightened, John began to pull the load aggressively along the ground. Yet, although it was not heavy, he found the task difficult. Something was still trying to drag the bundle back. He was obliged to turn around, face the bundle and haul it, as if he were competing in a tug of war.

Despite this strange incident, John planted the laurels and they grew into a fine hedge. Many years later, however, he was awakened at midnight by weird howling coming from the laurels. Thinking it might be the cry of a cat, he arose, opened the window and shouted, 'Go away!' The sound persisted, so he went to the kitchen window, opened it noisily and called out again. The sound grew louder. During all John's previous experiences, he had remained relatively calm but that night he went back to bed in a lather of perspiration. He knew of the Banshee being a harbinger of death and felt this disturbance had something to do with her. His aunt died two days later.

A Church of Ireland minister who was interested in astronomy and bee-keeping was among the later tenants of Killynon House. He befriended John and they often spent hours walking around the estate. When the rector and his wife moved on, John heard later that they had died within a week of each other somewhere in Munster.

The next occupant engaged a workman who would have been but a toddler when John had his eerie experiences and would not have known of them. One day this man was discussing the repair of a fence with John. He seemed to be nervous. Eventually he told John that he saw a man dressed in clerical attire walking through the yard the previous evening and entering a shed. The workman had followed him but found the shed empty.

The next resident at Killynon was a retired British army captain, a veteran of the Second World War. He lived alone, fended for himself, for two fine hunters and for a pair of young foxhounds. John had some of the stables rented for cattle at the time. On different occasions both the Captain and John saw a strange black dog around the stables, whose presence, even when lying down, disturbed the other animals greatly. Once, John's cattle were quite frantic, so he shouted at the dog to go away. It refused. John had reins in his hand and he lashed out at the animal.

'He simply vanished before my eyes and seemed to go down through the ground,' he said. Was this the same dog that had earlier interfered with the courting couple? If so, he was ageless.

Unexplained apparitions of humans and animals, noises and other strange happenings became part of Killynon House's history. One couple who rented it had been hoping to live out their years in the quietness of the Irish midlands. They stayed two weeks, leaving without explanation. A County Meath family beat that record – they stayed just one night.

Another occupant employed an estate manager who called with John one day, saying that although his master's car was parked outside, he could not get into the house to make an urgent telephone call. John went with him and tried to help. They feared that the owner may have collapsed inside.

A tractor mechanic who was working in the yard joined them as they walked around the house to see if they could gain admission by another door or window. Twice, a stone dropped from the roof and landed at their feet. Then, as they stood at a side-door, wondering if they should force it open, they heard loud banging on it, from the inside. It sounded like sledgehammer blows and the noise reverberated around the yard. John thought he saw and heard glass falling from an upstairs window but he could see no shards on the ground. The two men announced that they would delay no longer in such a weird situation and left, the manager having decided to ring the Garda Síochána.

Whether the Gardaí came or not, John could not tell, but at ten o'clock that evening, the manager arrived at his door in an agitated state, repeating the words, 'Oh, it's terrible.' When he calmed down, he told John how the mechanic had left some tools at the house and had returned to collect them, bringing his mother along for the drive. The manager had joined them and all three had driven to the house. The sounds inside were worse than before and they also heard loud sobbing coming from many parts of the mansion, but from one room in particular.

John went to his own gate and the mechanic's mother, 'a woman of responsibility', gave him the same account and said that she was terrified. He collected a torch from his house and told his brother he was going up to Killynon in the mechanic's car. His brother decided to go too. There was no room in the car, but he said that he would walk across the fields and they would all meet up in the yard.

John got into the car and they took off. When they rounded a bend in the long avenue and the mansion came into view, silhouetted against the night sky, there were sighs of relief, because lights were blazing in a number of windows. Their relief was short-lived, however. The course of the avenue left the house out of sight for a few minutes and when it reappeared it was in total darkness.

The group continued on to the yard where John's brother joined them. The men placed a long ladder against the sill of a window from which the mechanic and his mother said they had heard the most prolonged crying. John climbed up, shone the torch through the window but could see nothing. He tried opening the window and managed to raise the sash sufficiently to allow his smaller brother to squeeze through. The others admired the brother's bravery and waited apprehensively at the front door, which he said he would open from the inside. When he did so, they all trooped in and searched every corner of the house but discovered nothing unusual or out of place. The mystery of the missing owner had deepened.

They all departed, and in his bed that night John tried for the umpteenth time to figure out the reason for so many strange happenings at the Big House. He asked himself if there was any normal explanation for them or if they were a result of something that had taken place years before. If there had been some great tragedy connected with Killynon House, why did the lore of the countryside he knew so well not offer significant information? True, some stories hinted that the house had been built on an ancient burial ground. And there were suggestions that the happenings had to do with spirits of people who had suffered violent deaths. But there was no concrete evidence. John was still confounded.

Next morning he went back to the house and saw a blue station-wagon parked beside the Captain's car. It belonged to the Captain's daughter. She saw John approaching and came out of the house, asking him if he was a member of the staff. She told him how her father had taken ill at three o'clock two mornings previously and had made a telephone call to his doctor, asking to be admitted to hospital by ambulance. The hospital had contacted her in the west of Ireland and she had come and stayed by his bedside until he died of heart failure.

Saddened by the man's death, John was working in his garden the following day when two large stones, which he recognised as being part of the roof of Killynon House stables, landed beside him. Nobody could have thrown them such a distance. He began to wonder: potatoes, glass, now stones? Was he a target for some spirit of the Big House?

He and the people of Cloghan were even more confused when, in the early 1970s, there was an unexplained fire in the vacant Killynon House. Only a shell remained and this was cleared away in 1978, when John decided to tell of the events outlined above. He stressed that there had been many other unexplained happenings.

Author's note: I have gone into considerable detail with this story because the late John Sheehy was an intelligent man not given to fantasy or nonsense. This account has been corroborated by the editor of *Westmeath Topic,* with whom John discussed at length the events at Killynon House.

THREE

A TRAGIC WEDDING DAY

Charles Fort near Kinsale, County Cork, is the site of one of the most moving Irish ghost stories. The ruins of the imposing edifice stand at Rinncurran, near the fishing village of Scilly. Sir William Robinson, who also designed the spectacular Royal Hospital in Kilmainham, Dublin, was its architect. Built c. 1677, it was the main coast-defence of Kinsale harbour. Each century saw additions and it was occupied right up to the departure of the British forces from Ireland in 1922. Anti-Treaty forces burned it during the Civil War that followed.

A martinet, Colonel Warrender, was an early commander of the garrison. His daughter Wilful fell madly in love with a young officer. Some sources say he was a visitor to the pleasant nearby bathing resort of Summer Cove. Others claim he was Sir Trevor Ashurst, a subordinate of the Colonel's. For convenience, we will call him Trevor.

Well, the pair married, and like many military celebrations, the wedding party continued throughout the day. In the evening the young couple slipped away for a quiet stroll around Charles Fort. It is easy to imagine the idyllic scene as they strolled arm in arm along the ramparts, watching the sinking sun cast its path of red sateen across the calm waters beyond.

A sentry came smartly to attention and saluted as they passed by. He watched as Wilful and Trevor stepped on a pedestal to admire the scene on the inland side of the fort. He listened and heard Wilful express delight at the beauty of a flower she had noticed. Shaded by the high wall, its petals stood out against the dark green of the field below. The sentry presented his compliments and offered to climb down to pick the flower for her. Wilful was charmed, but the bridegroom was a little taken aback when the sentry suggested that Trevor would have to dress in his private's uniform and take his place on sentry duty. If the Colonel decided to make an inspection, the sentry reasoned, he would severely reprimand the soldier who had left the post unmanned. Trevor thought a visit from the Colonel was unlikely – after all, the man was enjoying himself at the nuptial celebrations – and he demurred, not relishing the thought of a knighted officer taking a soldier's place and wearing a private's uniform. But the appealing look in his new bride's eyes decided the matter for him, and he agreed.

Wilful giggled when she saw her husband dressed as a private. Then she watched the soldier as he clambered down the steep side of the fort. His agility amazed her and when he reached the flower and plucked it for her, she clapped her hands daintily.

Meanwhile, Trevor was feeling somewhat drowsy from the emotion of the wedding ceremony earlier and from the fine wine consumed during the celebrations that had followed. He dozed off – just when the Colonel decided to demonstrate to the men of the garrison that even on his daughter's wedding day he would not neglect his military duties. Yes, Colonel Warrender strapped on his belt, checked his pistol to see that it was loaded, placed his cap on his head and strode out to inspect the defences of Charles Fort.

He found everything to his satisfaction until he came to the sentry post where Trevor was snoozing. What was this? A sentry asleep? Unthinkable! The Colonel drew his pistol and shot the errant sentry dead. But when he moved closer, he realised that he had killed his new son-in-law. Alerted by the shot, Wilful turned at that moment and saw at a glance what had happened. With an agonised scream, she threw herself off the battlements and her body struck a buttress. Her death was instantaneous. An overwrought Colonel Warrender looked down from the ramparts. Already his daughter's white bridal gown was soaked in blood. The last of the sun seemed to sneer over the horizon and cast a dark red spear across sullen waters towards him. With a roar the Colonel

turned and ran to the seaward side, climbed
the battlements and leaped onto the rocks below.
A mighty wave came crashing in and took away
his body in its ebb surge.

The triple tragedy at Charles Fort was the
subject of many stories in the centuries that have
passed since that fatal wedding day. While the fort
was occupied, officers sometimes felt themselves
being pushed downstairs and having to struggle
against some force that kept dragging them towards
the battlements, even on calm evenings. This never
happened to soldiers. All ranks, however, reported
seeing the ghost of the beautiful Wilful walking the
battlements, dressed in a bloodstained wedding
gown, pale and distraught. Her eyes always staring
ahead, never moving unless they perceived a flower.
Even since the fort became a ruin, those stories
continue. They all conclude that after that day no
soldier ever fell asleep while on sentry duty.

FOUR

THE RETURNING FRIAR

FATHER MATHEW AND THE FRIAR OF RED ABBEY

In Cork, a famous priest initiated a temperance movement that, as the Pioneer Total Abstinence Association, eventually spread worldwide. Father Theobald Mathew (1790–1856) is a minor player in a moving Cork city ghost story of a returned clergyman. It tells of an old woman who visited the Blackamoor Lane Capuchin Friary on the evening of 8 April 1838. It was dusk and while she was praying fervently, she kept her eyes tightly closed. There had been a Benediction service earlier and the church was full of the pleasant but overpowering perfume of incense. The woman had been working hard all day and was tired and after a while she dozed off and slumped in the pew. The sacristan did not notice her when he arrived to lock the church doors for the night.

When the old woman awoke, she discovered her plight. She tried calling out, but soon realised her voice was too feeble to be heard through the stout doors. Sleeping in the church all night was her only option. In the confession box she found the cushion of the confessor's chair. She made a pillow of this, then stretched herself out on a pew and was soon asleep.

The church clock striking midnight awoke her. To her amazement, the candles on the altar were alight and the church was washed in a brilliant light, such that the candles alone could not have provided. Her awe turned to fear when she saw a fully vested friar arrive, carrying the chalice and paten, covered with purificator and pall, in the normal way for beginning Mass. He faced the nave and asked, 'Is there anybody to serve my Mass?'

In those days only males were allowed serve Mass and so the old woman demurred. In any event, she did not know the Latin responses. Nor did the friar seem to notice her presence.

He spoke again. 'Is there anybody to serve my Mass?'

Once more there was no reply.

When the question rang out a third time, the voice was louder and reverberated through the empty church. The old woman cowered in her pew.

After what seemed an age, the friar sighed, bowed his knee before the tabernacle and returned to the sacristy. The candles dimmed slowly before becoming fully extinguished. Frightened as she was, the old woman noticed that there was none of the smoke that normally appears when candles are snuffed out.

Throughout the remainder of the night she could not sleep and she felt colder than before the midnight intrusion. When the sacristan opened the church doors at six o'clock in the morning, she almost hugged him, so great was her relief. She told him nothing, but went directly to Father Mathew and related her experience.

The priest told her not to worry. 'Do not tell anybody about this. I can assure you, I will investigate it and put everything right,' he said.

That evening, Father Mathew sent the sacristan home early, saying he would lock up the church himself. He did so and began his vigil. Sure enough, as the candles lit and the friar emerged from the sacristy,

'Is there anybody to serve my Mass?' he asked.

Father Mathew did not reply nor did he do so at the second request. When the friar asked a third time, however, Father Mathew replied, 'I will.'

The friar smiled broadly and said, 'Then please come forward,' whereupon Father Mathew took his place kneeling on the step of the altar.

'*Introibo ad altare Dei,*' the friar intoned.

'*Ad Deum Qui laetificat juventutem meam,*' Father Mathew answered, and the celebration of Mass continued without incident.

Father Mathew noticed that the celebrant was extremely solemn throughout. During the

Consecration, he uttered every word with great concentration and never took his eyes off the Sacred Host and chalice. When the friar finally said '*Ita missa est*,' Father Mathew replied, '*Deo Gratias*,' and immediately asked the reason for the midnight visits. The friar told how he had once been a member of the community at the Red Abbey. He had always said Mass quickly and often was insufficiently aware of the awesome Sacrifice he was celebrating. When he died, his soul was banished to Purgatory until such time as he managed to celebrate the sacred office with due solemnity and reverence.

'You have helped me and I thank you,' he said. 'And now I go to behold that which I have so long yearned to see – the sight of heaven. When I pass through the Golden Gate and prostrate myself before the sapphire throne, my first prayer will be for whatever is dearest to the heart of him who has emancipated me.'

Father Mathew did not need time to think. 'Pray that I may be given the grace and the power to free my fellow-countrymen from the one degrading vice that, like a leprous spot, deforms souls that in many other respects are noble and pure,' he replied instantly.

The friar said, 'I promise,' and moved back into the sacristy. His Mass server followed, but the apparition had disappeared.

On the following day, 10 April 1838, Father Mathew signed a pledge of abstinence with the words 'Here goes, in the name of the Lord.' He began his crusade and within six years half the adult population of Ireland had joined 'The Pioneers' and revenue tax on alcohol almost halved. By then the Capuchins had left Blackamoor Lane but perhaps the paranormal spirit kept its promise.

Father Mathew extended his activities to the Irish population in England. After his death in Cobh, County Cork, on 8 December 1856, others continued promoting his total abstinence campaign and despite a changed society, the organisation still survives today.

FIVE

THE *GREAT EASTERN*

A mystery surrounding a ship launched in Millwall Dock in London in 1858 was solved in Dublin many years later. The *Great Eastern* had a total displacement of 32,160 tons and measured almost 700 feet. She had a double iron hull. Two sets of twin engines powered an enormous screw-propeller and paddles. And if all that was not enough, it had sails rigged on six masts. It was the largest ship in the world to be built in the nineteenth century and with a projected speed of 14.5 knots, a powerful prototype for fostering the technical possibilities of large iron steamships. Indeed, by the end of the century, steamships were well advanced in displacing sailing ships on global trade routes.

I.K. Brunel and J. Scott Russell had designed the *Great Eastern* for the Eastern Navigation Company to carry passengers and cargo between ports in Britain and India. So it was also the prototype of the ocean liner. At its launch, the Great Ship Company purchased it, and put it on a New York trade route. However, its gigantic cargo holds were only half full during the Atlantic crossings. After six years of deficit trading, the Great Eastern Steamship Company purchased the ship and used it as a cable-laying vessel until 1874. Two attempts at laying a successful transatlantic cable had failed. Each attempt had used two ships coming from either direction. The second attempt did succeed initially but communications broke down after a few weeks. The *Great Eastern,* due to the amount of cable it could carry, did the job alone. Some commentators said it was the most useful work it had ever carried out. But it had problems. The cable broke 600 miles from Newfoundland and it took a year to lift it from the seabed, at a depth of 15,000 feet.

The company interrupted cable-laying when the ship sailed from Liverpool to New York to attract American visitors to the Paris Exhibition. Eventually, the financial situation demanded that the vessel be relegated to sailing from port to port as an exhibition craft. It then went to the breakers' yard.

Economists have given many rational reasons for the failure of the *Great Eastern* but some people know differently. They whisper about a particular payday in 1857, during its construction. The hull was in position and the firm's paymaster came on board. Members of the crew were certain that they saw him arrive on deck with his payrolls and other documents. But he did not appear at his desk at the usual time. Nor was he ever seen again. There were rumours that he had absconded with the workforce's wages.

Seafarers began hearing stories. The ship had serious difficulties berthing in New York at the end of its major voyage. Soon after, she ran aground and the cost of refloating her was considerable. And there was the cable-breaking incident. In fact, on every voyage, something seemed to go wrong. As a result, sailors began to believe that the ship was haunted. Their stories persisted and spread, and soon her owners were finding it difficult to recruit men to crew the ship.

Shortly before it was broken up, the exhibition ship anchored in Dublin Bay. A clergyman attended a concert in one of its saloons. The performance did not appeal to him, so he took a walk around the deck. He met a man carrying a pile of documents and assumed that he was a clerical employee. The man looked pale – almost transparent – and was extremely thin.

The incident meant nothing to the clergyman until many years later. He attended a dinner party one evening with a friend, a retired maritime insurance executive who had been an officer on the *Great Eastern*. He told the clergyman about the commercial failure of the vessel, about the paymaster who had disappeared and about the claims that the ship was haunted. He vouched for the fact that sailors believed that the ghost of the paymaster appeared after every misfortune.

The clergyman paled and whispered, 'I think they may have been right. I may have seen the ghost.'

But the insurance executive's story was not over. He described the twin plates of the iron hull and how, in the breakers' yard, a smashed skeleton had been discovered between them. The paymaster had somehow fallen between the giant plates in one section just before they were pressed together. He had been crushed to death.

SIX

NELLY OF THE GLEN

The 1798 United Irishmen leader Michael Dwyer (1771–1826) evaded capture during the rebellion by hiding out in the Glen of Imaal in County Wicklow. The Glen has provided an artillery range for the British and Irish armies and Coolmoney Camp has featured in films, including *The Blue Max.* Coolmoney House stood above the camp proper. It served as an officers' mess until its demolition in 1999. Officers were reluctant to sleep in its haunted room, number 21a. This was not always due to fear of its ghost; colleagues liked to play pranks on occupants. A certain Director of Ordnance had no qualms about using it and he always got a good sleep – because each night before retiring he announced that he would keep a loaded revolver under his pillow in case he was disturbed.

Coolmoney House dated back to 1837 and it once belonged to the Hutchinson family. At that time the room that became number 21a belonged to a servant named Nelly. She became pregnant and a member of a local aristocratic family was said to be the father. Glen lore suggests that he arranged to meet Nelly in her room and then murdered her. He threw her body through the window into the basement below.

Officers and orderlies have vouched for the

presence of a dark stain on the floorboards of 'Nelly's room'. It was never possible to scrub this stain away. Indeed, maintenance personnel in the Engineers Corps have said that the floorboards were once replaced and that the stain reappeared on the new boards. Soldiers on duty late at night reported hearing strange sighing sounds and seeing a female form on the stairs. Old soldiers claimed that the room was sealed up in times past and that it was discovered when an officer inspecting the outside of the building noticed the extra window.

In 1999 the army finally demolished Coolmoney House. Not before it had attended to some unfinished business, however. On 15 February a chaplain, Father Declan Foley, conducted a prayer service, and he asked God to 'give peace to Nelly and to all who have experienced suffering in this house'. A wag suggested that the prayer would include many young officers who had endured hardship in the Glen. In a more serious vein, a local youth murmured, 'Everyone is at peace now.' And others present reported an eerie stillness, punctuated by intermittent cold breezes.

Ireland's national press reported the service, which was held in the finely plastered drawing room of the old Hutchinson manor. About forty local people attended and among them was a woman who had seen Nelly's ghost – Yvonne

Croke, the daughter of Commandant Kevin Croke, who was then in charge of Coolmoney Camp. As a child living in Baldonnel, Yvonne regularly talked to and saw her dead grandfather. Her father then got their house blessed by Father Ray Field, who later became Auxiliary Bishop of Dublin. And in recent years her mother, Colette, was travelling with her husband on a visit to her own mother in a Cork Nursing Home. Commandant Croke was driving fairly fast because the family had got word that the woman was seriously ill. Near the Jack Lynch tunnel, which brings traffic to the south-city, Colette told her husband, 'You can take it easy; she's dead.' And they discovered later that that was indeed the moment of death.

For some time before this, Yvonne had been suffering from a minor ailment. This ceased at the time her grandmother died.

But back to the Glen! A riding instructor, Yvonne was returning from feeding a mare at about five o'clock one Sunday evening, 7 February 1999. Although she knew nothing about the story of Nelly, she saw the form of a frail, gaunt young woman in the window of Coolmoney House. She told her father and three days later they both drove past the deserted house and saw the apparition. It was then that Commandant Croke decided to have the prayer service conducted before the house was demolished.

Yvonne attended the service, even though she was on crutches after an accident. She told me that she saw the same young woman sitting on the window-ledge of a large bay window of the officers' dining room. The apparition was behind the officiating chaplain. This time Yvonne got a better look and saw that the young woman was 'thin, pretty and about fifteen or sixteen years of age and about five feet six in height. She wore a full-length, plain, whitish dress with a dark belt around the waist and had shoulder-length, black, unkempt hair. She had a faded appearance and did not smile.' But the distraught expression Yvonne had noticed when she first observed the figure was gone. And so was Nelly – as soon as Father Foley ended the service.

The priest left the room to bless the remainder of the house, including the 'Ghost Room'. Those who had joined in the prayers followed. All except Yvonne. Because of her crutches, she could not climb the stairs. But she watched the ghost arise from the window-ledge and follow the priest as he left the room.

The demolition of Coolmoney House took place and the contractors set fire to the house timbers. However, Commandant Croke reported that the timber from Room 21a did not burn.

SEVEN

AT ARM'S LENGTH

One of Dublin city's many haunted houses stood in Mountjoy Square. Within its walls, residents, servants and guests experienced strange incidents. Objects fell from shelves, bedclothes were whipped off and tossed around rooms, and in the darkness a housemaid mysteriously suffered a sharp slap on the face. However, a visitor by the name of Major McGregor was able to shed some light on what had happened.

In the New Year of 1872 McGregor was a guest in the house. He had arrived from England at the end of the previous year. The husband of a relative fell ill and the Major volunteered to keep watch over him during the night. He did so for a few nights until the man seemed to be getting better. One evening the Major decided to retire before midnight but instructed the night footman to call if the patient needed him.

He was not long asleep when he awoke suddenly. Somebody was poking his shoulder. Assuming it was the footman, he asked what was amiss. There was no answer – just another jab, this time more urgent. The Major became irritated and said testily, 'Will you speak up, man, and tell me what is wrong!'

As there was still no reply, the Major moved his hand about in the darkness and clasped a hand – a

fleshy, soft palm. A woman's, he guessed, and he
held on.

'Who the blazes are you?' he demanded.
Silence.

So the Major attempted to tug the intruder
towards him. He failed. Although now somewhat
scared, he forced himself to speak once more.
'Who are you, Madam? Don't you know it is
improper to be in a gentleman's bedroom at this
hour?' At the same time, he moved his other hand
to the intruder's wrist and touched a frilly linen
cuff. Up along the forearm then, discovering heavy
velvet dress material. Then the clock struck but the
Major was dumbstruck. There was nothing to feel
above the elbow!

The Major released the hand and dashed from
the room. He ran to the patient's bedroom but the
man was sleeping soundly. The Major stayed the
rest of the night in the chair beside the bed.

Next morning, he told his story to the
footman, who laughed and said, 'So you are the

latest to meet the Master's Aunt Betty! The poor soul lived to a great age but died about fifty years ago.'

There was no theory as to why Betty's arm was abroad at night while the rest of her body was in repose. Keeping a wrist watch, perhaps!

EIGHT

CURSE OF THE CASSIDYS

Older natives of Monasterevin, County Kildare, alleged that a place known as 'The Weeping Ashes' was the birthplace of Father Edward Prendergast (1749–98), but people from Rickardstown also claimed him. He received his education in Salamanca, where he also studied for the priesthood and was ordained. Returning home, he became curate at Harristown. During a battle at Monasterevin in the 1798 United Irishmen Rising, he visited Barn Hill, where the rebels had camped. Local folklore tells how he only went to the area to baptise a sick infant. Whatever his motive, he was captured. On 11 June he was convicted by court martial and sentenced to be hanged.

Tradition claimed that a prosperous distilling family named Cassidy had the authority to save one person from the gallows each year, so Father Prendergast sent word to the distillers, seeking a reprieve. They refused.

Before he died, it was said that he placed a curse on the family, vowing that crows would soon be building nests in the malt-houses and that nobody named Cassidy would be left living in Monasterevin. So began 'The curse of the

Cassidys on you', a common Kildare/Carlow
malediction.

Father Prendergast was hanged from a tree
beside the River Barrow immediately after his trial.
The Black Horse Regiment guarded the priest's
body that night but, by arrangement, a friendly
yeoman supplied them with drink until they
became intoxicated. Captain Padraic O'Beirne,
a relative of the dead priest, led a small group of
oarsmen up the Barrow from Derryoughta. It was
a dark night but tradition has it that a mysterious
light directed their course. They seized the corpse
and brought it to a place called the Diver's Bush,
where they put it in a coffin and bore it to
Harristown cemetery.

People say that the guiding light appears each
year on the anniversary of Father Prendergast's
hanging and moves along the same route it
travelled in 1798.

NINE

COLLIER'S *'WEAKLY'* GUEST

Peter Fenelon Collier was born in County Carlow in 1849. In 1866 he emigrated to the United States and worked in a publishing house. Remaining in the industry, he eventually formed a company and began publishing religious material, particularly for the Irish-American, Roman Catholic market. He expanded into the lucrative magazine area and founded *Collier's Once a Week*, which first appeared in 1888, advertised as a magazine of fiction, fact, sensation, wit, humour and news. In four years it had a circulation of a quarter of a million and in 1895 it became the celebrated *Collier's Weekly*. When Collier died in 1909, his son Robert took over the running of the magazine and increased its circulation to the one million mark.

Robert Collier liked hunting and in the 1930s he came to Ireland for the hunting season. He stayed in the home of the Plunketts, Earls of Fingall, at Killeen Castle near Dunshaughlin in County Meath. Originally a medieval castle, the celebrated architect Francis Johnston had remodelled it in 1801.

Collier arranged a dinner party one evening but the hunting was good and he returned late.

He rushed into the castle to wash and change quickly so that he would be in time to greet early guests. While running through the hall, he saw a man approaching, dressed in a snuff-coloured tunic and breeches and wearing a powdered wig. Collier wondered if a guest had thought it was a fancy-dress occasion. As he walked to the man he held out his hand in welcome. The apparition glided towards him but veered suddenly and slid into the oldest room in the castle, Lord Fingall's study.

The castle contained portraits of Plunketts from earlier times. Many of them wore snuff-coloured clothes. Collier studied them closely but could not be certain that the ghost he had seen resembled any one of them.

TEN

THE 'GHOST ROOM' IN MAYNOOTH

There is a small green opposite the ruins of the FitzGerald Castle in Maynooth, County Kildare. Through its ancient trees runs the short driveway leading to St Patrick's College. An Act of the Irish Parliament established that institution in 1795 and within a century it became the largest seminary in the world. From 1286 the green in front of the college was a market place and a gallows site. Up to sixty people were hanged there and the ghosts of some have been reported in the past. In later years some seminarians from distant parts sold their horses there on arrival. No paranormal activity in this historic area has been documented to the same extent as the 'Ghost Room' in the college itself, however.

If a visitor to the college stands between the swimming pool and the power-house and looks southward towards Rhetoric House, he can see where a window has been filled in. It is in the centre of the row of windows in a small wing protruding in his direction. This is the window of the 'Ghost Room'. A clerical student from County Limerick committed suicide in the room in 1841. He slashed his throat with a razor. Some accounts claim that before he died he leaped through the window. Nineteen years later another student did the same thing. They say he was mentally disturbed.

An abundance of stories have been told about the room. One tells how a student was shaving when he noticed a figure standing behind him, miming the drawing of a razor across the jugular vein. Thereafter, occupants kept their razors in a ewer filled with cold water, in case the tragic victims had acted in their sleep. There is also a claim that a priest's hair turned snow-white the morning after he had kept a vigil in the room when the second death occurred. Other reports mention a charred mark on a floorboard in the shape of a cloven hoof and bloodstains that were impossible to remove.

The second suicide took place on 20 April 1860 and a resolution of the college trustees dated 23 October 1860 suggested 'That the President be authorised to convert room No. 2 on the top corridor of Rhetoric House into an oratory of Saint Joseph'. The window was blocked up and the wall into the corridor was knocked down. A niche remained for the statue of Saint Joseph. The President at the time was Doctor Charles Russell, who wrote letters about the incident. The Vice-President and Professor of Scripture, Doctor Daniel McCarthy, had attended the young Kilmore student for three days while he was dying in the

Junior Infirmary. He recorded in his diary how the young man admitted to being in deep depression for a considerable period before his suicide attempt. The Coroner's Jury stated that he 'Died of his own hand, being of unsound mind at the time'.

Doctor Tomás Ó Fiaich, later Archbishop of Armagh and Cardinal, made a study of the 'Ghost Room' while he was President of the College. He claimed that there were in fact three suicides. Two students had cut their throats and a third had leaped from the window. Some claim that the story about students placing their razors in ewers began with the last death. The shock of the cold water jolted the young man into a realisation of what he was about to do, and thus prevented him from cutting his throat. He did jump out the window, however. Some say he was seriously injured, but survived. Despite Doctor Ó Fiaich's research, there is still doubt about whether he lived or died.

In 1977 a bedroom adjacent to the oratory became a chapel of meditation but bedrooms remained on the other side. Five students occupied them in 1978. They were Joseph Gallagher (Raphoe diocese), who had returned from New York to study for the priesthood; Donal Kilduff and John Curtis (Kilmore diocese); Brendan and James Walsh (Kerry diocese). Not one of them reported any unusual disturbance in or about the oratory.

Maynooth College now has an excellent visitors' centre in the care of an informed and attentive woman. Callers admire the College Chapel on the north side of Gothic Square. Lucky researchers who gain admission to the Russell Library are similarly impressed. In the College Museum's collection are induction coils used in experiments by Doctor Nicholas Callan, who invented the coil that led to the modern transformer. Despite all these attractions, visitors are still inquisitive about the infamous 'Ghost Room'.

ELEVEN

PERSONAL TOUCH

THE HAUNTING OF AYLMER CASTLE

Donadea in north Kildare is now a popular forest park. I played in its demesne as a child, watched an Italian firm producing charcoal from its fallen trees, and enjoyed games of table tennis in the Aylmer Castle tower. The castle has a long history. In 1558, Richard Aylmer of Lyons received the manor of Donadea from the Earl of Ormond. Richard settled it on his second eldest son, Gerald, an ardent supporter of the Catholic cause, which he pursued relentlessly at the court of Queen Elizabeth. In 1622 he was created Baronet of Donadea by King James I. Other Aylmers were prominent in the north Kildare area. William Aylmer, from nearby Painestown, became Colonel of the north Kildare army of the United Irishmen, and gradually imposed discipline on his recruits. After the opening battle of the rebellion at Prosperous, he established a camp in an area surrounded by bogland near Timahoe and held out there with up to 3,000 men. When the force eventually surrendered, it was suggested that family friendship with the Marquis of Buckingham averted his execution.

Those matters meant little to me in my childhood. If I happened to leave the castle after dusk I was fearful, because the grand Lime Avenue leading from its eastern gate was haunted, locals claimed. A coach pulled by four headless black horses and driven by a headless servant in navy livery with brass buttons, delivered beautifully dressed ladies and foppish gentlemen to the castle at regular intervals.

The castle itself was haunted too. Before it fell into ruins, a strange smell pervaded its walls. Its grand entrance hall was dark and chilling – certainly to a child. In 1938 *The Irish Times* reported what people from Staplestown to Hortland had known for years – that a lady in a white crinoline dress walked its stairs, corridors and drawing room. Some had seen her and had felt themselves forced to step aside to give her space to pass. And when she did, the observer felt a ripple of ice-cold air.

Only one person ventured to suggest whose ghost she might be. He claimed that a guest at a grand ball in the castle had moved upstairs to view the gathering below. She leaned too far over the banister and fell down the stairwell.

PHANTOM CAR

One Sunday night in 1969 I retired to bed in my
Mullingar home. I had to drive to the Curragh
Camp in County Kildare for an urgent meeting at
nine o'clock on Monday morning. My sleep was
erratic and I was fully awake at six, so I decided to
begin my journey and try to get some rest when I
reached the Curragh. Between Edenderry and
Rathangan I heard a loud clanking sound at the
back of the car. A hubcap had come loose, I
assumed, so I stopped. There was just enough light
to inspect the road in search of a hubcap – if I
were missing one. But I was not. All four were
firmly in place. Dawn was breaking and the
stretches of bog on either side of the road were
covered in a low mist. All was silent until I
distinctly heard a car starting up and moving away.

An aural illusion? Could I possibly have heard
the sound of a car on the nearest parallel road
about three miles away as if it were beside me?
I doubt it.

SCARE AT ANNAGHMAKERRIG

While tussling with a play script many years ago, I
visited the quiet artists' retreat of Annaghmakerrig,
Newbliss, County Monaghan. This was once the
home of the distinguished actor, author, director
and producer Sir Tyrone Guthrie (1900–71). I had
intended staying a few days. On the third night

I awoke to the sound of a shriek from the door. A figure dressed like a harlequin, with a pale mask-like face, was leaning in through the door and laughing raucously at me. Then the full form came through and bolted across the room, emitting a shrill whirring sound, and disappeared through the window. I was terrified. Was it a nightmare? I do not think so.

In a conversation next day, the director of the centre, Bernard Loughlin, happened to inform me that I was sleeping in the room where Guthrie had died on 15 May 1971. He also told me that all the occupants of the house, with the exception of budding playwright Jim Nolan and myself, were going to Belfast that evening and would be returning late. By the time they had left I had decided that I could not spend another night in the house. I made Jim aware of my decision, and he decided to leave too.

I wrote to Bernard and apologised for my hasty departure but did not disclose my reason. If he reads this in his new Spanish home he will understand why I never returned to Annaghmakerrig.

TWELVE

BRIEF ENCOUNTERS

SAINT MALACHY

One of the oldest Irish ghost stories goes back to the era of Saint Malachy (*c.* 1094–1148). It tells how the saint disavowed his sister in Armagh because she lived a life of abandon and spurned religion. She died while he was in Lismore, County Waterford, and he offered Mass for her soul each day. As time passed, he neglected the practice. One night he had a vision in which an angel told him that his sister was standing in the porch of the monastery. 'She has not eaten for thirty days,' the angel said. Malachy then remembered that he had not offered Mass for her soul for thirty days. He robed and went to the church and began Mass. Through the glass in the door he saw his sister clad in a grey robe. He prayed to God for her and then saw her in a cream-coloured garment, inside the door of the church but unable to approach the altar. Again Malachy prayed for his sister and her robe became a dazzling white. She walked to the altar, with a smile on her face.

BLUE LADY OF ARDS

A Stewart family had a home in idyllic surroundings near Creeslough overlooking

Sheephaven Bay in County Donegal. It later
became Ard Mhuire, a Capuchin monastery where
80 per cent of Irish Capuchins studied. A feature
of its original interior architecture was a pair of oak
staircases. Each one ran along a facing wall, leading
from the vestibule to join a long landing above.

A ghost story connected with the house tells of
a young friar's surprise when he saw a beautiful
young woman dressed in blue standing at the top
of one staircase. A common Irish superstition claims
that bad luck will follow a couple who meet on a
flight of steps, so the friar crossed over to the other
staircase and began his ascent. Again the woman
appeared. The friar returned to the first staircase
and once more faced the woman. At that stage
he decided to ignore the superstition and began
climbing. He met the woman halfway and she
seemed to pass through him.

Locals recalled that at one time a window of
the original house had been blocked up, but no
one knew why. Some claimed that it belonged to
the Blue Lady, who was a Stewart, but could not
offer any background to explain her appearances.
They all agreed, however, that other priests and
staff admitted to seeing the woman in blue in a
number of locations throughout the monastery.

There is disagreement about why the nocturnal
visits ended. Some alleged that an exorcism took
place, others claimed that the friars became quite

67

BRIEF ENCOUNTERS

fond of the friendly ghost and were sorry that the
Blue Lady discontinued her residence in
Creeslough.

The Stewart house was demolished in 1966
and Ard Mhuire is now modernised and free from
ghosts.

HOTEL CHILD

A man named Martin Burke leased three Dublin
houses in 1824 and opened a hotel that was to
become world famous. The Shelbourne Hotel on
St Stephen's Green had the Empress Elizabeth of
Austria as a guest in 1879 and its patrons down the
years included the tenor John McCormack, the
Dalai Lama, the Queen of Tonga, Laurel and
Hardy, John Wayne, Princess Grace of Monaco,
James Cagney, Peter O'Toole and Richard Burton.
Michael Collins chaired a committee that drafted
the first Constitution of Saorstát Eireann there.

The hotel had another guest, however, whose
name did not appear on its register. Staff who
worked in the warren of workshops beneath street
level, repairing furniture, stocking wine and
laundering linen, knew her. She was a young girl
who appeared on occasions always looking ill and
worried. Gossip suggested a number of theories.
Was she the spirit of a child who had been
murdered? Or an orphan abandoned by a wealthy
but uncaring guest?

One account holds that the girl's name was Mary Masters, that she was a victim of the cholera epidemic in 1832 and that she had lived in one of the houses that became part of the original hotel. The daughter of a woman whose maiden name was Masters stayed in the Shelbourne Hotel in 1965. This woman, Sybil Leek, was reported to have contacted Mary in room 256 or 526 (over years, even ghosts get their numbers mixed up!).

HOTEL GUEST

A house set in the foothills of the Antrim plateau was once the abode of the mayors of Carrickfergus. One occupant, a lady named Elizabeth, became romantically involved with a soldier of the garrison at nearby Carrickfergus Castle. A tunnel linked the two buildings and she began using it whenever she visited the castle to meet her loved one. Her husband found out and one night he lay in wait for her at the tunnel, and killed her. Knowing that her lover would be waiting at the other end of the tunnel, he moved swiftly through. The soldier got more than a fright when, instead of his beloved, he met her raving husband, who beheaded him.

In local tradition, Elizabeth was known as Maud and her lover, Buttoncap. Today, Dobbin's Inn occupies the site of her house and employees have spoken of seeing Maud when they were cleaning up after a late night. She wanders through the building, wringing her hands and looking distraught.

WINDOW BEADS

Iveagh House on St Stephen's Green was once the home of the Guinness family (Earls of Iveagh) but it now houses the Department of Foreign Affairs. Following a Good Friday custom in times past, people prayed on the footpath in front of the building. They were waiting to see the imprint of a set of rosary beads that appeared occasionally on a pane of glass in a certain window. The custom dates back to an incident when a Roman Catholic servant girl asked permission to go to the local church to kiss the cross. This religious practice involved visiting the church and kneeling before the altar where a brass crucifix would be left lying on a cushion. At three o'clock, the hour of Christ's death, the faithful would kiss the hands, feet and face on the crucifix.

The girl held her rosary beads in her hand and tried to explain how important it was for her to go. 'It won't take ten minutes, sir,' she promised.

When the master refused, the girl became distraught. She cried and pleaded with him to such an extent that he lost his temper and began shouting at her. Still she begged him until, in a mighty rage, he whipped the rosary beads from her and flung them at the window. The utterly shocked girl dropped dead at the horror of what he had done. Ever after, those beads appeared in the window on Good Friday.

NOT A MAJOR BLUNDELL

Granard, County Longford, is renowned as the home of Kitty Kiernan, the hotel proprietor who was the girlfriend of Michael Collins. It suffered severe damage during the rebellion of 1798 and in the War of Independence (1916–21). J.P. Farrell, who compiled *Historical Notes and Stories of the County Longford* in 1886, described an early British garrison in the town as being 'the most ungovernable corps in the British service'. Captain Blundell was in charge, a man who was 'the cream of the service … in dress, manners, sporting propensities and general recklessness'.

At a grand ball in the officers' mess, Blundell charmed the ladies throughout the evening. Next morning he did not appear on parade. This surprised his colleagues because he was punctual by nature and had always prided himself on playing well and soldiering well. When he still had not appeared by lunchtime, they wondered wryly if he had escorted a lady home, or if he had perhaps imbibed too heavily – something they considered most unlikely. Eventually they went to his room and found it locked. They examined the window from the outside and saw that it too was thoroughly secured.

After considerable discussion and argument, they decided to break into the Captain's room. To their horror, they found Blundell's body lying on the floor behind the door and his bloody, severed head seemed to stare at them from beneath the bed. It could not have been suicide. Nor murder, because the door and windows had been locked from the inside. What had happened then?

No one ever discovered the answer, but plenty of people in Granard claimed to have observed the ghost of the headless Blundell, mounted on a black horse and riding through the town at the midnight hour.

DRAMATIC ENTRANCES

Dublin's theatres have their own ghosts – not all of them playing Hamlet's father! Fishamble Street Theatre became famous for the first public performance of Handel's *Messiah* in 1742. It was then open but a year and was better known as Mr Neale's Music Hall. On a wall in its green room, knocking began at precisely ten o'clock each night and lasted for a quarter of an hour. No reason for the phenomenon was ever given.

A number of back-stage personnel at the Olympia Theatre in Dame Street attested to seeing a man in costume wandering in the wings. An actress believed the man was watching her performance one night. When she made her exit

and approached him to introduce herself, she
bumped into the wall and the man disappeared.
Others claimed to have seen a glowing light moving
up the stairs to the dressing rooms. This light may
have been the troubled soul of a man who was on
the run during the Civil War (1922–23). He took
refuge in the theatre but was discovered and shot
dead by his pursuers while trying to escape. Some
reports claim the man's name was O'Donovan.

For decades, theatre folk have spoken about the
Grey Lady of the Gate Theatre. One of the most
recent sightings was in the wardrobe department,
when the Earl of Longford's company was in
residence. As a wardrobe assistant sat sewing, she
thought she saw Lord Longford's late wife
Christine entering the room, clad in grey silk.
When she looked closer, the lady disappeared.
In June 1971 Brian Phelan's *The Signalman's
Apprentice* was playing. Everybody had gone home
and the caretaker was on his rounds switching off
lights, before locking up for the night. He was
surprised to see what he thought was an actress
still in costume standing in an open dressing room
doorway. He asked her to hurry. At that moment,
the light on the stairs went out. The hair on his
head must have been standing on end as he
returned downstairs in darkness. He waited a while
at the stage door but no one came down the stairs.

When Monto, Dublin's red-light district in
Montgomery Street, was flourishing, the city's
high-class brothels were called 'flash houses'. They
attempted to reproduce the *ambience* of the
celebrated Chabanais in Paris – the 'House of All
Nations' founded by an Irish woman named Kelly.
One 'flash house', incongruously called the Maiden
Tower, stood in Fishamble Street. Its madame was
also named Kelly, and known as Darky. Officers of
the law from Dublin Castle carried out many
'inspections' there and were reported to have
dallied an unseemly length of time. Simon Luttrell,
a Sheriff of Dublin, has been named as the father
of a child born to Darky Kelly. Allegedly, Darky
murdered the baby. Luttrell was the prosecutor at
her trial. She was executed, although the body of
the baby was never found. Its ghost walks this
historic area of the city, especially in the vicinity of
St Audoen's Church. Folklore hints that the infant
is seeking a priest to baptise it.

The ghosts of some of the prostitutes, dressed
in the finery worn when they drove around the city
in coaches displaying themselves to prospective
clients, also appear in this area from time to time,
as do the spirits of destitute wretches, including
lepers.

NEGATIVE VALUES

A feature by Dara deFaoíte (author of *Paranormal Ireland*, Dublin, 2002) in *Ireland on Sunday* on 27 October 2002 reported on a 1989 visit by an English tourist, David Blinkhorne, to the sixteenth-century tower of Thoor Castle, near Gort in County Galway. W.B. Yeats lived there in the 1920s and it is where he wrote his collection *The Tower.*

Mr Blinkhorne received permission to photograph the drawing room in the tower. When he collected the developed photograph, he was shocked to see in it the figure of a young boy. He checked with the pharmacy which had processed the film and was told there was no fault in the developing – the image was definitely in the negative.

Lady Gregory, a colleague of Yeats, lost a son in the Great War. At a seánce, Yeats believed that he had contacted a boy who had committed suicide by hanging. Dara deFaoíte speculated on the latter as being a possible source of the image in the film.

ON THE SPRITE TRACK

The area around Slieve Gullion in County Armagh is rich in folklore. One of its many ghost stories is unusual, as it concerns a train. Near a place called Aghavalloge, the Dublin–Belfast line curves to avoid Carn Hill and the Camlough Mountains to the north. About the year 1912 a gatekeeper at a level crossing heard a train approaching one night. It was not on his schedule but he still did his duty by lighting his lantern and standing at the road that crossed the line. The train emerged from a cutting known as 'The Wellington' near Meigh, passed him and continued on to Barney's Bridge, where it disappeared. It was fully lit but he saw no passengers on board. A check with his superiors in Newry, nearly five miles north, assured him that no train was expected.

The gatekeeper began to wonder if he had experienced a hallucination, but a few nights later he was at home playing cards with a few men when the same thing happened. This time there were witnesses. No one could explain the phenomenon and there were no further sightings for some time.

When the Troubles broke out in Northern Ireland and bombs on the line became a regular occurrence, stories about the ghost train began to resurface. People claimed that it appeared before an imminent crash or if a bomb had been placed on the line.

MONASTIC AFTERLIFE

Speaking in 1997 to Pauline Jackson, author of *Ghosts of Cork* (Cork, 2001), Mr O'Flynn, the proprietor of the Franciscan Well Bar in the North Mall of the city, claimed that he had experienced phenomena such as a sudden drop in room temperature, sounds of dragging footsteps, closing doors and objects smashing in the bathroom. He contacted a local priest who concluded that the perpetrator of the disturbances was 'a friendly but mischievous poltergeist who was probably trapped'. The priest blessed the building and things became quiet. Mr O'Flynn believed that the poltergeist was a monk, because the bar was located on the site of a monastery belonging to the Franciscan Medieval Community.

HUGH LEONARD'S EXPERIENCES

The playwright Hugh Leonard told me about strange experiences he had. His mother died in May 1965 and not long afterwards he had an experience that he described in detail to his wife, Paule. She put it down to a dream, but, although he had been in bed at the time, he disagreed. Some years later, they saw a programme on BBC television about 'out of body' experiences. Paule recognised that this is what her husband had experienced in 1965.

'I am not at all what is called "psychic",' Hugh

Leonard added, when he finished relating this episode.

He had further strange experiences after Paule's death. The first occurred on a Monday about eight months after her demise:

I had been working upstairs and needed to check on the spelling of a surname in *The Irish Times*, which was in the downstairs living room in a small pile of papers for recycling. I went downstairs quite briskly. I recall that I was not thinking of anything except the work I was doing. As I entered the living room, I was facing towards the window, where the papers were, and I instantly became aware that Paule was standing in front of the unlighted fire and facing away from both the window and me. She was very vivid and wearing her smartest dressing gown. Her hair which, [in her final years] she had dyed blonde, was bright gold. She vanished instantly, for all the world as if she were a trespasser and I had come upon her unexpectedly. Or as if I were tuned into a certain wavelength and the connection were broken. There was nothing that suggested an illusion, this was, as I say, utterly vivid. She was there.

Several months later – Kathy [an American woman] was staying with me by then and was in the bedroom – I again had occasion to go downstairs for something or other. As I did so, Paule walked past the bottom of the stairs. This time, she was grey – as if faded – and almost transparent. It was as if her spirit was wearing out and would soon be gone.

There was a third experience, on a cruiser in France – Paule loved cruising. I will not talk about this; it was a very sweet experience and extremely personal, and it upsets me to write about it.

LATE LATE EXPERIENCE

Radio Telefís Éireann's *Late Late Show* on Friday 15 November 2002 devoted considerable time to discussing the 'out of body' experiences of people who believed they had seen the 'other side'. One woman in the audience, identified as Majella, told how she was having a massage one day when she noticed a vivid white light in the window of the room. Then she discerned the form of what she believed was an angel. She felt her body getting heavy, yet it seemed to be rising from the massage couch. Everything seemed beautifully bright and serene and, with the angel, she ascended into a clear blue sky. Then she saw her father and the angel told that her father was going to die. But Majella called out, 'Love, you stay longer.' He smiled and disappeared. She was in such a beautiful place that she wanted to remain there.

Majella then felt the masseuse nudging her and telling her that a neighbour had telephoned to say that her father had suffered a heart attack. When Majella got the details and checked timings, she realised that her father's attack occurred while she was on the massage couch. He had been taken to hospital in an ambulance but the paramedics had to carry out emergency resuscitation – at the same time as she was having her out of body experience. She believed that by calling out to her father, she had saved him.

PARANORMAL.COM!

Ghosts have entered the world of technology. A website, Irelandseye.com, tells about the ghost of Helena Blunden, a young linen worker in a Belfast mill. She made a wax cylinder recording of 'Pie Jesu' from Fauré's *Requiem* on 24 January 1912 and was killed in a fall three months later while at work. The recording and newspaper reviews pertaining to it were found in a bundle of linen discovered in 1999. The website invites visitors to listen to it. A printing company then occupied the old mill. Its employees experienced eerie encounters with a ghostly inhabitant believed to be Helena. They also heard unexplained footsteps on corridors and on stairs.

THIRTEEN

LETTER IN A LIBRARY

Nestling behind a small gate in St Patrick's Close, beside St Patrick's Cathedral in Dublin, is Archbishop Marsh's Library. Narcissus Marsh (1639–1713) was born in Hannington, a small Wiltshire village. After studying at Oxford, he was ordained in 1662. He held a number of appointments before becoming Provost of Trinity College, Dublin, in 1679. At Trinity he played a significant part in preparing Bishop William Bedell's (1571–1642) Irish translation of the Old Testament for printing. Marsh served in Ferns and in Cashel and was enthroned as Archbishop of Dublin in 1694. Jonathan Swift (1667–1745) held Marsh responsible for his celebrated 'penitential letters' and for hindering his promotion within the Church of Ireland.

A bachelor, Marsh occupied the Palace of St Sepulchre, with his niece, nineteen-year-old Grace Marsh, acting as housekeeper. This was a depressing situation for a spirited young woman in a fashionable city. Particularly since the Archbishop was attempting to turn her mind to scholarly pursuits. He was building up his collection of books and establishing one of the first three public libraries in Europe within the grounds of the palace. He chained readers to their desks to prevent the theft of books.

On 10 September 1695, Grace eloped. Marsh recorded in his diary: 'This evening betwixt eight and nine o'clock at night my niece Grace Marsh (not having the fear of God before her eyes) stole privately out of my house ... and (as it is reported) was that night married to Chas Proby Vicar of Castleknock in a tavern and was bedded there with him – Lord consider my affliction.'

His affliction was exacerbated by the fact that Marsh believed Grace would at least have left a note of apology for her action. He searched in the library, believing that it was to be found in one of its thousands of books. His ghost continued to do so after his death.

The pair were finally reunited: Grace died in 1770 at the age of eighty-five and was buried in her uncle's tomb. Among Marsh's private collection is a book titled *Lachrimae Lachrimarum, or The Distillation of Teares Shede for the Death of Prince Panaretus* (London, 1613) by Joshua Sylvester. Its endpapers bear the inscription 'Grace Marsh Her Booke 1689'.

FOURTEEN

THE KERRY DANCES

Wild and romantic, the area around the western edge of Ballinskelligs Bay cossets one of the last Irish-speaking communities in County Kerry. The remains of a MacCarthy castle stand on Ballinskelligs Point and, nearby, centuries of fierce Atlantic breakers have ravaged Ballinskelligs Abbey, once a priory of Canons Regular of Saint Augustine. Tradition states that it housed the monks of the Great Skellig when they withdrew from their ocean-battered monastery. There are remains of wedge tombs, ogham stones, anchorite cells, clocháns, souterraines and many other archaeological wonders in the surrounding countryside.

This is perfect ghost country and the Rider of the Red Gap gallops occasionally along the shoreline between the Red Gap (An Bearna Dearg) and the MacCarthy castle. Over 2,130 years ago, a man named Daniel Cremin was gathering kelp on a moonlit night and loading it into panniers slung across the back of a mule. The animal suddenly took fright and bolted and, according to Michael Kirby, author of *Skelligside* (Dublin, 1990), 'You could hear the blasts of superfluous gas exploding from the animal's rear end, as it struggled and strained its way up through the soft sand.'

Then Daniel heard the sound of a horse in full gallop – hoofbeats, snorts, creaking leather and the lashing of a riding crop. Something sped past, scattering great piles of seaweed and driftwood until they became silhouetted against the moonlit sky like storm clouds. A solid man, not easily frightened, Daniel crossed himself and returned home. The mule was there ahead of him, the panniers intact. But it was sweating profusely.

Kirby reminds his readers of other happenings in the area. Night and day, horses passing the Turn of Starts (Pluais na bPreab) near Kilreelig were inclined to bolt. If pulling a cart or trap, the driver always alighted and led the horse past.

A woman had a habit of bittling her clothes on a flagstone near a bridge over the Ballinskelligs River. No one ever saw her, but a number of people who heard the sound tried to reach the spot it came from. However, it always remained a distance ahead.

FIFTEEN

THE DEVIL'S KITCHEN ABOVE KILLAKEE

There were strange happenings when, in 1970, a television crew attempted to film around Killakee House in the Dublin Mountains. They wanted to follow up a story reported by a journalist in a Dublin evening newspaper, concerning a crippled hunchback and a giant black cat which jointly haunted the vicinity of the house and the notorious Hellfire Club on the rise above it. But while they were having a tea break, their cameras and other paraphernalia moved.

William Conolly (1662–1729), Speaker of the Irish House of Commons, built a hunting lodge on Mount Pelier. Reports suggest that in clearing a site he removed a cromlech and that the pagan gods it commemorated brought bad luck to the inhabitants of the house. Conolly's lodge later became a centre of activities for Dublin's 'bucks', who relished this piece of lore. These were the arrogant and vicious members of Georgian Dublin who engaged in hedonistic pursuits, including fornication, blasphemy, gambling, drunken orgies, Black Masses and other Satanic practices.

In May 1735, Richard Parsons, first Earl of

Rosse, James Worsdale and Colonel Jack St Leger founded the Hellfire Club, whose motto was 'Do as you will'. Famous among its members were Buck English, Buck Sheehy and Buck Whaley (senior and junior). While the Mount Pelier lodge was an occasional meeting place, members more frequently used a local hostelry called the Eagle Tavern and Daly's Club in the city. One account of their behaviour at the Eagle tells how members sat around a table bearing a large punch bowl of steaming *scailtín*. They toasted Satan and called for 'Damnation of the Church and its prelates'. Then they poured the hot whiskey over a cat and set its fur alight. The distracted animal leaped screaming through the window and ran flaming around the mountainside. Since that night, occasional sightings of the spirit of the burning cat, darting through the furze and heather, have been reported.

The wealthy Richard Chappell Whaley, a descendant of Oliver Cromwell, was president of the club when Mount Pelier was burned. He was known as Burn-Chapel because of his detestation of all religions, especially Roman Catholicism. On the Sabbath he would mount his horse and ride around the Dublin Mountains with a torch, lighting the thatch of churches. His colleagues regarded him as a pyromaniac.

After a Black Mass at Mount Pelier, members engaged in a drunken orgy, during which a waiter

stumbled over a comatose body and spilt whiskey over Whaley. The furious buck abused the fellow, then poured liquor over him and set fire to his hair and clothes. In a terrified attempt to quench the flames, the unfortunate waiter tore a tapestry from the wall and tried to wrap himself in it while he was running down the stairs. The tapestry took fire. Its blaze leapt to other drapes and pieces of furniture and soon the house was engulfed in flames. The drunken bucks perished, all but Whaley. He and a few members of staff escaped by jumping through a window.

Subsequently, the club was almost inactive until a son of Whaley's, Thomas, revived it to 'defy God and man in nightly revels'. These activities included homosexual and heterosexual orgies, gambling and Black Masses. Thomas Whaley was a heavy gambler who won £25,000 from the Duke of Leinster by riding to Jerusalem and back within a year, and £12,000 by jumping a horse from the third-floor drawing room of his home in St Stephen's Green onto the pavement below. The horse was killed but Whaley survived and eventually became penitent.

While praying in St Audoen's Church one day he saw Satan approaching him, and he fled, not just from the church but from Ireland. He spent the last few years of his life with his mistress in the Isle of Man. His abode was later known as Whaley's Folly. Sclerosis of the liver killed him at thirty-four years of age and his writings warned young people that a 'life of dissipation can produce no enjoyment, and that tumultuous pleasures afford no real happiness'.

Stories of apparitions at the Mount Pelier premises of the club and at Killakee House, and of ghosts moving between each location, have always been part of Dublin lore and the barn-like ruins of the Hellfire Club, silhouetted against a night sky, with scudding clouds lit by moonlight, can indeed be an eerie sight.

A retired Garda officer, Nicholas O'Brien, and his wife, Margaret, lived in part of the original Killakee House which had been converted into an arts centre. From the outset, there were problems. Tradesmen employed at the refurbishment left, complaining about ghosts interfering with their work. About 1968, when the place had become inhabitable, three visitors departed hastily after seeing a crippled hunchback appear and turn into a black cat before vanishing. Margaret O'Brien reported seeing an Indian gentleman accompanied by two nuns strolling through the house. As there had been reports of two nuns appearing in the old tower and sprinkling holy water around the place, she arranged an exorcism. Things became quiet for about two years. Then other visitors held a séance and bells rang out, lights began flashing.

The television documentary filmed at Killakee featured the clairvoyant Sheila St Claire performing the automatic writing of which William Butler Yeats had been so fond. Through it, she claimed, she was communicating with the spirits of Killakee – spirits that soon were to make their presence felt.

Nicholas O'Brien went to Cork to visit his mother. While he was away, his wife heard noises each night and discovered that articles in locked rooms had been moved and, in some cases, damaged. These included heavy furniture and crockery. In a bar attached to the arts centre, pictures, bottles of liquor and an electric fire were smashed. In one area, everything was broken except a small bottle of holy water. Margaret told of hearing an unidentified dog barking and of its howl being taken up by other dogs in the neighbourhood.

Her cats disappeared and were later discovered in the old tower, which was securely locked.

Father Settelle, a priest who had heard about the events at Killakee and who had experience of such things on the Continent, visited the O'Briens. He believed that Sheila St Claire had contacted poltergeists and, by doing so, had upset them. He also warned against admitting strangers to the house.

Sheila St Claire had a warning for the O'Briens too. She told them to remove the brass image of a cat from a door in the arts centre. There is no confirmation that she directed them to another brass ornament, one which had been attached to a painting of a giant black cat that hung in the cold stone hallway but was missing. It was later discovered in an old holy water font in one of the rooms. Also in brass, it was an image of Satan.

SIXTEEN

LADY OF THE LAKE

> To the south is the lovely Lough Ennel
> Where Malachi's island doth rest
> Rooks and pigeons now call
> 'Round the old Jealous Wall
> It's a spot that is fifty times blest.

A song in praise of Lough Ennel in County Westmeath never hints at a story that a witch from the west placed the lake in its present location south of Mullingar. An anonymous poem, however, tells how the witch filled her *práiscín* with water from the Shannon and, flying around the midlands, noticed a 'hideous bog [within] sloping hills and woodland fair':

> Then pausing in her airy flight
> 'This is the spot,' she cried
> And soaring to a dizzy height,
> Her *práiscín* she untied.

'The water fell in beauteous spray and when the scene was clear', she added islands and other attractive features and called the lake Ennel. Perhaps its mythological beginning had something to do with a ghost story associated with the lake.

A man named Brendan L'Estrange was walking by the lake's Dysart shore at nightfall when he was taken aback by the sight of a slim woman dressed in dark clothes paddling in the water. It was late in the year and the water must have been very cold, he thought. Then the woman began gesticulating wildly, as if she were reprimanding the lake. She shouted something he could not understand, then hurried out of the water and away, disappearing into the dusk.

L'Estrange spoke to a few people about the incident but they thought there was nothing unusual about it. Not until a man on the Carrick side of the lake noticed the same woman a few days later. This time she was seen wearing a bright blue cloak and wore a veil. All the other details agreed with L'Estrange's account. On this side of Ennel stood the Jealous Wall built by Robert Rochfort (1708–72), Earl of Belvedere, so that his brother Arthur, whom he suspected of being his wife's paramour, would not be able to see his fine Belvedere House. People began wondering if this was the ghost of Lady Belvedere, whom Robert eventually locked up in Gallstown House, a good three miles away.

The man who saw the woman at Carrick, Matt Gallagher, spoke about his experience in his local pub. People listened, word spread and soon there were sightings of the woman at a number of places

around the lake. In every account she was slim and
beautiful, paddling bare-footed, and gesticulating
angrily towards the water. Only the colour of her
dress or cloak changed. She became known as the
Lady of Lough Ennel. Her appearances were such
a frequent topic of conversation that groups of
young men went to the lake shore for the sole
purpose of trying to spot her. But she only
appeared to lone wanderers or fishermen who
were not expecting to see her. Jack Tuite of
Dysart, for example, had a closer encounter than
most. When he saw the woman, her clothes were
bright and illuminated in some way. She was
smiling, and instead of disappearing, she
approached him and spoke.

'At the bottom of the lake lies my treasure,'
she said. Then she vanished, and nobody ever
reported seeing her again.

The lakes of the midlands are steeped in
folklore. Lough Derravarragh is associated with
the story of the Children of Lir. Below Lough
Suedy in Ballymore lies the original town of
Ballymore and legend tells that Lough Owel, where
Malachy drowned the Viking chief Turgesius,
covers a city. But there had been no mention of
any treasure lying beneath Lough Ennel, until
Tuite's report. There have been suggestions that the
woman lost someone dear to her in the waters of
the lake. Others believe that the apparition is the

ghost of Lady Belvedere, who may have been out boating and lost some precious jewels before her incarceration. Ennel was once Europe's premier fishing lake – the record weight for a brown trout is 26 lb 2 oz, caught by William Meares on 15 July 1894. A keen angler has suggested that the spirit was referring to Ennel's enviable stock of wild trout, and an entrepreneur has recently suggested that there may be oil or a lode of gold below the bed of the lake. Perhaps the witch who fashioned Lough Ennel dropped something more than water from her *práiscín*.

Whatever the Lady of Lough Ennel was referring to, the lake can still be a quiet, peaceful place in the evening, despite frequent invasions by water scooters and speed boats and loud, uncaring visitors.

SEVENTEEN

THE DEVIL AND THE DAUGHTER OF LOFTUS HALL

Hook Lighthouse in County Wexford is one of the oldest operational lighthouses in the world, dating from the early thirteenth century. Included in its fine visitors' centre is a condensed history of Loftus Hall nearby, which tells of an incident that is similar in many ways to another tale of the devil's appearance at Castletown House, County Kildare.

The remains of Loftus Hall can be seen on the seaward side of the approach to Slade village on the Hook peninsula. Redmond Hall stood on the site from 1350. In 1666 the Loftus family acquired the mansion and gave it its present name.

In the eighteenth century, Charles Tottenham lived in the mansion for a while. He became MP for New Ross in 1727. In 1731 he was at home when he heard that the Irish Parliament was proposing to vote its surplus of £60,000 to Westminster. He mounted his horse and galloped the 110 miles to Dublin Castle. Mud-spattered from head to toe, he dashed into the chamber still wearing his riding boots. The Speaker overruled angry protests on grounds of protocol, and

Tottenham's vote defeated the motion. Thereafter, he was called 'Tottenham in his Boots'.

One stormy evening, sheets of cold rain were sweeping across the desolate Hook peninsula, while Tottenham and his family were sitting comfortably in front of a blazing wood fire. Through the howling gale, they thought they heard the clatter of horse's hooves approaching outside. Then there was loud knocking on the door. Tottenham opened it and found a stranger tying a black horse to the foot-scraper. The man begged shelter for the night, and although apprehensive, Tottenham agreed. He was soon glad he had admitted the stranger because he proved to be a good conversationalist and was a perfect guest in every way. There were few things that Tottenham liked better than good company and a convivial atmosphere, so he brought the best wine from his cellar and his wife prepared a fine supper.

After the meal, the family played cards and during the game, one of the female family members happened to drop a card under the table. When she stooped to retrieve it, she saw the stranger's cloven hoof. Her screams could be heard in Slade as she stood pointing at the man and shouted 'It's Beelzebub! It's Beelzebub, I swear it!'

And she was right! The stranger slapped his cards on the table and before anyone could shout 'Snap!', he became enveloped in a cloud of purple smoke and disappeared through the ceiling. He seems to have made his final exit through one of the chimneys, because it was found shattered the following morning and all attempts at repairing it failed.

There were other disturbances at Loftus Hall during Tottenham's occupation. At one of his many lavish parties his daughter met and fell in love with a handsome young man of whom her father disapproved. The relationship developed, however, and eventually the young man proposed. Tottenham refused his daughter's hand and ordered the young man never to call at Loftus Hall again. Furthermore, he refused his daughter permission to leave the house at any time.

Her life became a monotonous hell, her daily routine consisting of walking the corridors, slumping drearily in the drawing room *chaise-longue*, or languishing in her bedroom. Eventually she became ill, but her father remained adamant that she would not see her lover again. Bereft of any will to live, the young woman soon succumbed to her depressive derangement and died.

Immediately after her funeral, servants at Loftus Hall began to report sightings of her ghost. Wearing a distraught countenance, her slight, beautiful form, dressed in white, began wandering through the mansion, just like the lovelorn young woman had done during her cruel confinement.

Some versions of the story have the young woman falling in love with the handsome Satanic card-player. They say that after his hurried departure she went mad and began to ramble forlornly about the house.

In any event, Charles Tottenham eventually called in a local priest, Father Thomas Broaders, to perform an exorcism and neither the Devil nor the wandering woman appeared at Loftus Hall again. Father Broaders later became parish priest of the twin parishes of Ramsgrange and Hook. He died a canon in 1773 and was interred in Horetown cemetery, where an inscription on his final resting place, now almost illegible, reads:

> Here lies the body of Thomas Broaders
> Who did good and prayed for all
> And banished the Devil from Loftus Hall.

Loftus Hall fell into disrepair but in 1870 the fourth Marquis of Ely demolished its ruins and began constructing a new three-storey mansion with nine bay windows and a parapet with balustrade. It was completed within a year. Interior features included a magnificent oak staircase and panelling. Benedictine nuns occupied it from 1917 to 1935 and the Rosminian order was housed there from 1937 until 1983, when it became a hotel. Mikie and Kate Devereux were the most recent residents. Mikie died in 1993 and Kate was still living alone there in 2003.

EIGHTEEN

THE KILLING KILDARES

No collection of Irish ghost stories would be complete without a tale of the Pooka. This phantom animal appears in folklore in a number of guises and colours: donkey, horse, large cat, goat, bull or dog, in white or brown but most often in jet black. W.B. Yeats introduced it as an eagle and some stories describe the spirit as a voluptuous young woman. Many believed the Pooka to be Satan. Its eyes were often described as fiery red with flames shooting from them. At Hallowe'en, adventurous children went 'out with the Pooka', but many more stayed indoors, fearful of the stories they had heard of infamous pookas and how these creatures spat on blackberries and made them poisonous.

A huge black dog stood sentinel on the bridge that takes the Foxford–Castlebar road across the river connecting Lough Con and Lough Cullin. There were similar pookas in Ballaghadereen, County Roscommon, and in Ballygar, County Galway. The Kildare pooka was a donkey which did the work of a kitchen maid, and a pooka from Derry appeared as a horse that terrified anglers. The White Spirit of Béal na Méine (Mouth of the

[River] Maine), associated with a spot near Castlemaine, County Kerry, appeared as a blinding white light and was a female devil who brought two people to their deaths. Perhaps the most famous manifestation, however, is the animal spirit that gave its name to Poulaphuca (Hole of the Pooka), where the River Liffey becomes the county boundary between Kildare and Wicklow. It is the site of a hydro-electric power station, where the river flows through a narrow gorge before plunging 150 feet in three stages. A pool under the second drop is the Hole of the Pooka.

In November 1813, before the present bridge was built over the gorge, the Kildare Hunt, known as the Killing Kildares, lost its pack of hounds at this spot. The meet had partaken of the traditional stirrup cup at the Tipper crossroads, near Naas. It failed to raise a fox until it approached Tipperkevin, north of Ballymore Eustace, where a large specimen took a course towards the Liffey. At the same time, a black horse appeared, unmounted, and the huntsmen did not recognise it as belonging to any of their riders. Nor did they see it for what it was – the Pooka.

A quick check revealed that all who had set out from Tipper crossroads were still present. The terrain was difficult and the fox ran fast, so that, approaching the Liffey, only a lone huntsman named Grennan and the Pooka remained with the

pack. The gorge was in full spate but the hounds
were gaining on their quarry and began picking
their way across rocks. Grennan realised the danger
and attempted to recall the hounds, but the Pooka
went dashing ahead, so urging them to continue.

The fox headed for the narrow part of the
gorge where the bridge now stands. There was a
ledge on either side. The fox hesitated for a second.
Then it looked back and saw the approaching
Pooka's red eyes spitting fire. The fox attempted
to leap across and almost made it. Its front paws
reached the opposite ledge but it failed to drag
itself up and fell into the turbulent waters below.
The Pooka leaped across the gorge easily and
disappeared into the woods beyond, but the pack
of hounds, hard on the scent of the fox, went
headlong into the pool.

Grennan moved up to the ledge and, looking down, saw the fox and the hounds trying desperately to swim to safety through the swirling, foaming swell. And he saw some hounds dashed on jagged rocks, yelping in pain and dying. He wept as he watched most of the pack going under and he shed a few more tears when the fox eventually made it to the other side. His sorrow gave way to terror, however, when he heard a diabolical neighing – as though an animal were laughing – from the woods opposite.

There are other versions of this story, including a comprehensive account that appeared in the *Sporting Magazine* for 1832, which described an outlandish route taken by the hunt.

The account given here is from a Kildare man who, in the 1930s, sadly stood above the valleys of the Liffey and the King's River and wept, like Grennan, at the sight of so many humble homes which would soon be submerged forever by Blessington Lake, created to supply water for the power station at Poulaphuca.

NINETEEN

SPIKE ISLAND'S GAUNT GUNNER

A Coast Defence Artillery unit of the Irish army occupied Spike Island in Cork harbour. Its transport for bringing visitors from the pier, where they had disembarked from the steamer *General Mac Hardy*, to the officers' mess was a rather decrepit truck. It has been said that the driver was beyond retirement age but remained in service courtesy of a powerful friend from his youth – Eamon de Valera. During formal functions, it was amusing to see this soldier helping ladies in beautiful ball gowns up a wooden ladder to sit on hard seats in the rear of the lorry. When the dancing ended, officers often told these women about the soldier ghost of Spike Island, which some called the Gaunt Gunner, and jested that they might meet him on their way back to the pier.

The tale begins when the British army gunners occupied the island. The young daughter of a serving soldier, Eileen by name, went down to the pier each morning to collect a newspaper that the skipper of the steamer brought over from Cove (later Cobh) for her father. Her path passed the medical officer's house, which was surrounded by a high wall. A rich growth of mature shrubs and garden trees tumbled over it. One dark grey morning Eileen was startled to see a human face peering through the foliage. Although the weather was dry, the face appeared to be wet and, most frighteningly, it had no eyes – just two dark holes above the nose.

Then more of the body appeared, in military uniform, and to the young girl's horror, it slithered over the wall and came towards her. She screamed and ran back towards the married quarters in the garrison, taking shelter in the first house she came to. A woman there consoled her, but then informed her that a number of people had seen the apparition.

Under the Anglo-Irish Treaty, British troops withdrew from Ireland in January 1922 but the coast defences, including Spike Island, remained in their hands until 1939. However, as some soldiers were evacuating the island on 21 March 1924, landing at Cobh, they came under machine-gun fire and one soldier was killed. This fatality has been linked to Eileen's story, although there is no connection. However, an Irish soldier and one of his superiors had an unusual experience that evoked the shooting.

The soldier was on guard duty one night when someone approached his beat from the direction of a disused store near the guardroom. He called out, 'Who goes there?', and got no reply. The figure came forward and, as required, the sentry called twice more and warned that he would fire if identification were not forthcoming. By now he could see that figure approaching was in British army uniform. Still it advanced and the soldier fired.

The orderly officer heard the shot and hurried to the guardroom. The sentry told his story but, since there was no body, he felt rather foolish. The officer considered charging the soldier for firing unnecessarily, but he had heard about the Gaunt Gunner and decided to keep watch with the sentry when next he was on guard duty. This he did and saw the same figure emerge from the disused store. It approached in slow march. The officer drew his pistol and fired but the figure continued to advance and seemed to walk through the officer before disappearing. Both the officer and the sentry were shaken by their experiences – especially next day, when the building from which the Gaunt Gunner had emerged was discovered burned to the ground. A Court of Inquiry was unable to establish the cause of the fire.

TWENTY

GHOST FAMILY FESTIVAL

Richard T. Cooke, founder of the Irish Ghost Family Festival (*see* Introduction), has written and lectured on ghosts. He grew up in the late 1950s early 1960s in the North Mall section of Cork city, an area renowned for ghostly sightings. On 15 November 2002, I interviewed him.

'We were surrounded by ghosts, none of which I saw myself,' he said.

He spoke of hearing about ghostly figures of nuns walking in the playground of an old building called the Rock School (now the Blarney Street Community Association Centre) and about figures of monks around the Franciscan church site and its cemetery.

'It was not unusual, during a wake, for bereaved members of the family to engage in conversation with their loved one who had died and whom they could see sitting up in the bed smiling back at them,' he said.

His mother laid out corpses for wakes and was often called upon to console a friend or neighbour who was having trouble with the spirit of a loved one recently deceased.

'I remember going along with her to visit one particular woman, a neighbour of ours,' he recalled. 'Her late husband, to whom she was devoted, had been buried for some time but his spirit began sitting by the open fire in his old chair, smoking his pipe and dressed in his work clothes.'

The woman could hear his footsteps around the house and doors banging. Strangest of all for a spirit, the outside toilet flushed regularly and water taps ran. Cooke's mother, he claimed, spoke to the spirit. Her understanding assistance, together with the services of the parish priest from St Mary's Church in Pope's Quay, brought peace to the distraught widow.

Aggie Begly was a neighbour of the young Richard Cooke. Of low stature, she had snow-white hair and always wore a black shawl over a blue and white polka-dot bib. Punctuality was her forte and, running from house to house in her fur-lined boots, she obliged all early risers by calling them each morning. When Aggie passed on to her eternal rest, she was greatly missed. But only for a while, because shortly afterwards, those whom she had called in life continued hearing knocks on their doors at the appropriate hour. They also said they saw Aggie walking along the terrace.

When Richard was about ten or eleven years of age, his cousin died and after the obsequies, the mourners repaired to the Franciscan Well, a pub on the North Mall. Richard began to pass around an old coffin handle he had picked up in the cemetery. His Uncle Abey, who had travelled down from Dublin for the funeral, chastised him, saying he should not have taken it from the 'home of the dead'. Abey and Richard's father drove him back out to St Mary's Church in Curraghkippane and made him leave the handle where he had found it. Shortly after that Richard had a personal experience which recurred twice in his later life. This is his story.

Growing up beside the River Lee, which to us kids was like the Mississippi, offered endless opportunities for adventure. Just like Huckleberry Finn and his friends, we used spend our days fishing along the North Mall. Many times I ventured out on my own and it was on one of these occasions that something strange occurred. While I was fishing from Vincent's Bridge I slipped and fell into the water. I wasn't a very good swimmer then and even if I was, the current was far too strong and fast for me to swim in it. As I struggled to save myself, I suddenly saw a lady's smiling face in the water. The next thing I knew I was sitting on one of the slip steps on the North Mall, five hundred yards from where I had fallen in. To this day, I do not know how I got onto that slip. There was nobody around to help me and it would have been impossible for me to pull myself out of the water because the current was dragging me down.

This would not be the last time I would see this smiling face. On one occasion about nine years later two friends and myself were on a punt in the middle of Lough Mahon late in the evening when it capsized, throwing us all overboard. As I struggled to take off my clothes and heavy boots that were making me sink like a stone into the depths of darkness, the same smiling face appeared to me again, after which thankfully I was able to swim to safety along with my two friends.

Again, in the mid-1970s the smiling face appeared to me but this time it was in a tunnel of white light. This was a near death experience which occurred to me after I had collapsed with a burst appendix. I had completed a recording of my music in the RTÉ studios in Union Quay, Cork, when I had to be rushed to the North Infirmary Hospital. After I regained consciousness a day and a half later, the doctor informed me that had I been any later coming to the hospital I would have died.

Cooke's own experience led him to study paranormal happenings and he visited numerous places where sightings and other unusual occurrences had been reported.

'I interviewed people of all ages and from a variety of backgrounds who told me of profound supernatural experiences and apparitions they had witnessed,' he said.

In the early 1980s, while he was attending University College Cork (UCC) Cooke was working one day in the Cork Archives Institute in Christ Church. Religious services had been celebrated in and around this building and people had been entombed there for over one thousand years before it was deconsecrated in the 1970s. Into this historic place arrived a man who helped Cooke understand his own experiences. Michael Campbell was a burly, bearded American, wearing heavy-rimmed glasses. He smiled broadly and said he had taken time out of his lecturing schedule at UCC to consult some of the documents that interested him.

As Cooke was giving him a brief history of the building, Campbell suddenly said, 'You have a lot of friends.' Cooke agreed. But his guest was not referring to human friends. 'He had in mind the spiritual friends that inhabited the building, which he saw all around me,' Richard said. He continued:

> I was taken aback by what he had said because he was acknowledging what I had been experiencing and encountering on numerous occasions since I was young. Michael was a holy man with a wonderful sense of liberty that captured me as he spoke openly about the

spirits, which surround all of us. He went on to introduce me to these spirits and then asked me would I like to introduce myself to them, which I did. Doing so was like taking a weight off my shoulders. An overwhelming sense of freedom and security washed over me. It was as if I could float. Our encounter on that day and our subsequent meetings would leave a lasting impression on me, for Michael gave me more confidence and belief, encouraging me to use the gift of communication I had. He showed me his own method of communication that brought me back to my dear mother, a gentle, honest, humble soul who used more or less the same approach with the many friends and neighbours who came to her. Over the years, people with similar issues have come to me and I have used my communication skills to help them.

One speaker at Cooke's inaugural convention was Helen Barrett, the White Witch of the Isles, a woman internationally known for her psychic abilities. When he mentioned his meeting with Michael Campbell, Helen Barrett informed him that Campbell was a wizard of the highest order.

The enthusiastic Irish Ghost Family Festival organisers hope to bring the event to Dublin and to other locations as their venture becomes more firmly established.

TWENTY ONE

MISTRESS AND SERVANTS

A Cork city haunting appears in Peter Underwood's *Gazetteer of Scottish and Irish Ghosts* (London, 1973) and also in Pauline Jackson's *Ghosts of Cork* (Cork, 2001). The story is said to be based on a true incident which occurred around 1873 in a fashionable district close to the city centre. In its retelling I take some licence.

In the household staff of a wealthy widow named Bishop were two good friends, Andy O'Leary, a jack of all trades, and Amelia Jenkyns, an orphan maid. Mrs Bishop had a fine wardrobe and every morning she dressed extravagantly to meet some friends for coffee in the city's best hotel. Amelia loved looking at her mistress's garments and sometimes she would hold one against herself and waltz around the room. She was particularly fond of a red dress with large buttons and a dainty collar, and was holding it against her body and looking in the mirror one day when Mrs Bishop returned early and strode into her boudoir. She was furious and reprimanded Amelia severely. The girl was particularly frightened by an evil look in her employer's eyes.

Mrs Bishop moved her most exclusive clothes,

including the red dress, into a wardrobe in another room which had always been kept locked. Andy and Amelia had often wondered about the room and about their mistress's late husband. What was he like? How did he die? Through their mutual interest in the mystery, their relationship blossomed and they fell in love.

One day they asked the milkman about the family and he told them that Mr Bishop had been very wealthy and much older than his wife. The couple took an annual vacation in the fashionable French Riviera. In fact, that was where Mr Bishop was buried. These details intrigued Amelia and Andy. Their young minds began thinking all sorts of things about Mrs Bishop. Especially after a vivid dream Amelia had one night. In the dream she saw her mistress take a key from a panel beside the fireplace in the drawing room. The woman then went to the locked room and opened it. She did not notice her inquisitive maid on tiptoe coming behind. Amelia tried to slip into the room but her mistress slammed the door too quickly. All the girl had time to see was a large four-poster bed. She tried peeping through the keyhole but a flame leaped from it and burned her eye, at which point she awoke.

Coupled with the milkman's information, the dream stimulated Amelia and Andy's young imaginations. They did not dare mention certain things that crossed their minds, even to one another, but they did discuss one possible explanation for the locked room. They believed that their mistress kept a hoard of money there, and thought that if they could lay hands on some of it, they could elope together. So when Mrs Bishop went out for coffee each morning, Amelia and Andy searched around the drawing room for the panel that held the key to their future. They did not succeed in finding it.

One evening Mrs Bishop went out to dinner. The pair of young servants were in the kitchen talking about all the things they had never seen or done because they were poor. Amelia said she would love to go on a cruise. Even a visit to Dublin would make her happy.

'Imagine, I've never been to the theatre,' Andy said.

With an impish smile, Amelia answered. 'Well, I'll do a bit of acting for you.'

Amelia ran upstairs, leaving Andy below wondering what she meant. She went to Mrs Bishop's room, whipped off her clothes and dressed in a beautiful silk gown, a large picture hat and elegant, high-heeled French boots. Then she went to the dressing table and made up her face with powder and rouge. She returned to the drawing room and cavorted around for Andy's amusement. Then she began acting out her dream. As Mrs

Bishop had done, she went to the same spot beside the fireplace and, lo and behold, a small panel opened. The delighted couple took the key and dashed to the locked room.

Amelia's hand trembled as she put the key in the lock and turned it. The door opened and they looked around in awe. There were two chairs ornately carved, a large safe and a full-length, gold-framed mirror. Despite her intense curiosity about the safe and its contents, Amelia could not resist looking at herself in it. Only then did she notice the bed behind her – the same big four-poster that she had spotted when she tried to follow Mrs Bishop in her dream. But there was somebody in it!

She gasped and turned around, clutching
Andy's arm and pointing at the bed. Lying there
was an old man with silver hair and a bushy
handlebar moustache. Before they could say
anything, they heard a creaking sound from a dark
corner. There stood a high, dark-stained cabinet
they had not noticed until that moment. Its door
was opening slowly and a woman was stepping out.
It was Mrs Bishop, wearing an elegant blue evening
gown and a magnificent diamond necklace, gold
bracelets and an assortment of rings. She was also
wearing the evil look that Amelia had seen in her
eyes the day she was reprimanded. The woman
moved quietly to the bed, took up a pillow and
pressed it down on the man's face.

The transfixed maid and handyman heard a
muffled groan and saw the woman kneel on the
bed and place the full weight of her body on the
pillow. Amelia screamed and suddenly the old
man and his attacker disappeared, leaving a cold
chill in the room.

Andy looked at Amelia. Neither had to state
the obvious – that they had witnessed a re-
enactment of a deed they had each quietly
suspected: the murder of Mr Bishop by his wife.

When they recovered from their shock, they
remembered their original intention in visiting
the room. But because of what he had witnessed,
Andy was reluctant to steal anything.

'Then I'll do it,' Amelia pouted.

She had difficulty opening the safe but eventually the door swung back. There were piles of gold sovereigns and boxes of expensive jewellery inside. She put on necklaces, brooches and bracelets and filled her apron's duster-holder. She stuffed her pockets with the gold coins.

'Now, let's go away to the south of France,' she said to a bewildered Andy, but he shied back behind the door.

'Oh, no you won't, you thieving little bitch,' thundered the voice of Mrs Bishop, who loomed up in the doorway. She ordered Amelia to take off all the jewellery and replace it in the safe. And all the while, Andy slid further behind the door, completely concealing himself. 'Now turn out your pockets, you slut!'

Amelia obeyed.

'And take off my clothes and get back into your own filthy rags.'

Mrs Bishop frogmarched Amelia to her bedroom and waited at the door while the girl sobbed and put on her own clothes. When this was done, Mrs Bishop grabbed Amelia's arm viciously and dragged her downstairs and out into the street. Andy heard them go and followed them at a discreet distance. A full moon gave plenty of light and he became very frightened when he saw the two women turn into a narrow lane that led to the River Lee. His heart was breaking as he heard Amelia's loud cries for mercy. Mrs Bishop dragged her charge on to a yacht moored at the Coal Quay and pushed her into the cabin.

Andy was perplexed. He knew he would be unable to overcome Mrs Bishop and even if he did, she would tell the police about Amelia's attempted robbery, to which he was an accomplice. He crept up to a porthole and peeped in. Amelia was on her knees and Mrs Bishop was choking her with a length of cable. The sight of his lover's puffed face and dilated eyes horrified Andy. So did the demonic leer in Mrs Bishop's eyes. But he still felt unable to intervene and in a daze he returned to the house and began attending to his night chores. Later he heard his mistress returning.

Mrs Bishop spoke to him in a relaxed manner, as if nothing had happened. 'Amelia has run away, Andy. I caught her dressed in my clothes and chastised her. But she is an orphan with nowhere to go. No doubt, she will be back soon.'

Andy made no reply. He kept his secret for about a fortnight, when he confided in the grandmother of Elliot O'Donnell, for whom Andy ran errands. She passed on this story to Peter Underwood.

The woman found it difficult to believe him, yet she knew he was a decent and sensible lad and was unlikely to concoct such a tale. After much soul-searching, she informed the police, who questioned Andy and Mrs Bishop. Mrs Bishop told them that Amelia had run away and that she had often done so before. In the nineteenth century the word of a wealthy widow would always be heeded before that of a servant, and so the police took no further action.

During dredging work on the port some time later, workers discovered the body of Amelia Jenkyns. Identification was possible, but due to the advanced stage of decomposition the authorities were not able to ascertain if she had been strangled or had drowned.

Cork people who rambled out of doors on the night of a full moon have reported seeing Amelia's ghost wandering along the quay. Sometimes she was wearing a servant's uniform – black dress, socks and shoes with a white apron and hair band. On other occasions she was in orphan's rags. At all times, her face was swollen and her dilated eyes were filled with horror.

TWENTY TWO

THE MAN IN THE YELLOW HOUSE

Rathfarnham, County Dublin, boasts a castle built by Archbishop Loftus around 1585, when he was Lord Lieutenant of Ireland. In 1641 it was a stronghold from which Sir Adam Loftus helped to defend Dublin against incursions from the O'Tooles and O'Byrnes, who inhabited the Wicklow Mountains beyond. A skirmish took place in the village during the 1798 United Irishmen rebellion, and a number of insurgents were killed and taken prisoner. By that time, a thatched cottage bearing the name the Yellow House was the village pub. Its licence dated back to the early eighteenth century and it stood on the site of the present Roman Catholic church, beside today's popular bar and restaurant of the same name. This building was erected in 1825 and it opened for business two years later. Distinguished residents of Rathfarnham would have frequented it, such as: John Philpot Curran, father of Robert Emmet's sweetheart Sarah, W.B. Yeats, the artist Sean Keating, and Eoin MacNeill, scholar and patriot. In 1979 the Yellow House was enlarged and extensively refurbished.

The inn had always been a popular meeting place for organisations of all sorts. A ballad, first

published in *A College Miscellany* in December
1921, aimed at attracting Trinity College students
to join the membership of Dublin City Harriers:

> If happy you desire a bath – the Yellow House
> Rathfarnham
> Has upon its kitchen floor a steaming tub
> And no longer need a fellow go unwashed thro'
> term for darn him!
> He can join the Harriers and pay his sub.

Without entering the bar, a room on the third
floor of the premises was accessible by flights of
stairs, landings and a corridor. This was the
meeting place of Dublin and District Motor Cycle
Club. The club organised a number of high profile
events including the Skerries 100, which took place
on the first Saturday in July. The event enjoyed the
goodwill of the property owners along its circuit.
In the 1960s, on the Wednesday before a race, its
organising committee met in the usual room of the
Yellow House. A keen enthusiast, J.H.R. (Harry)
Lindsay, and his colleagues, were shocked to hear
that a new property owner on the circuit, a Belgian
national, was objecting to the race. Entries had
been received, services and facilities had been
booked, so this objection constituted a major crisis.
There was only one hope – Harry Lindsay should
leave the meeting immediately and drive out to
Skerries and try to change the Belgian's mind. He

gathered up his papers and left the room.

Interviewed in November 2002, Lindsay said:
'I walked down the first flight of stairs, along its
landing and then down the second flight to the
landing before final flight. Above it, there was a
tall window and because it was July, there was
plenty of light.'

Coming down the final flight to the exit
passage, Lindsay saw a man standing against the
newel post. When he was about a foot from the
man and beginning to walk around him, Lindsay
uttered some greeting like 'goodnight'. But the
stranger disappeared. He did not walk away.
Nor did he fade away. He vanished suddenly.

'I did not experience fear. I was calm. The
way I felt seemed to extend beyond fear. It was
outright disbelief and I just kept saying to myself
"This just cannot happen",' Lindsay recalled.

He had seen something incredible but was about
to hear something stranger still. Down the stairs
behind him trooped the other committee members.
They were surprised to see him and asked if he
shouldn't be halfway to Skerries by now. They told
him how they had conducted business for a half-hour
after Lindsay had left the room – thirty minutes of
his life that Lindsay has never been able to account
for.

Lindsay described the apparition as being about
six feet tall, of slight build, with tight black curly

patches of hair on his head. A long coat hung
on him, reaching almost to the ground.

The rest of the week was hectic. Lindsay met
the dissenting Belgian and the Skerries 100 took
place as planned. A short time later Lindsay asked
the foreman at the Yellow House if there had been
any reports of the house being haunted or the like,
but the man had never heard of anything unusual.
Then Harry went on with his life.

If he was not afraid that night in the Yellow
House, Lindsay got a start many years later.
Travelling in a Dublin taxi one day, the hair began
standing on the back of his neck. The driver he
had hailed had the identical appearance of the
apparition he had seen years before. When he
collected his wits, he ventured to ask the driver
if he knew the Yellow House. 'I hear it's a great
place for a meal,' the driver told him, but no,
he had no connection with it whatsoever.

On his way to Bangladesh on business some
years later, Lindsay was listening to the radio in his
hotel room at London's Gatwick Airport. In a
discussion on the paranormal the presenter invited
anyone who had an unusual experience to phone
in. Lindsay rang the number but the programme
was over before he contacted its researcher. An
eminent professor, this man told Lindsay that the
half-hour time lapse he had experienced was
indicative of a genuine paranormal experience.

Time passed and the incident had almost left Lindsay's mind. Still enjoying his passion for motorcycling, he spent hours restoring vintage models at his home in Lacken, County Wicklow. One evening he was having a conversation with a couple of friends. As a young girl, one of them used to visit her grandfather, a veterinary surgeon who lived about 100 yards from the Yellow House. She frequently stayed with the family who lived over the pub and she told Lindsay: 'I used sleep in your clubroom. The owner of the house, a woman, was a bit odd.' She often heard this woman walking up and down corridors and stairs at night, and remembered making enquiries and hearing that the woman had a habit of walking alone around Rathfarnham village but holding a conversation with someone unseen. The part of his friend's report that most interested Lindsay, however, was how the woman always began and ended her conversations by saying 'hello' and 'goodbye' – at the exact spot where he had seen the apparition in the Yellow House.

TWENTY THREE

THE HEART'S A WONDER

Close to Ballyduff on the Lismore–Fermoy road stands Glencairn Abbey. The Glenmore River meets the Blackwater at the picturesque spot and it is not surprising that an exile – even one of tender years – would wish to be laid to rest there.

At the end of the eighteenth century, long before the Cistercian order of nuns purchased the estate, a wealthy family occupied Glencairn House. A young daughter fell ill and her doctor advised her parents that a sunny climate would benefit her health. Her mother, therefore, took the child on a European tour. They visited France and Spain and Italy, but the girl's health still deteriorated. By the time they reached Rome she was too weak to do any sightseeing, and she begged her mother to bring her home.

'Glencairn is more beautiful to me than any of these places,' the girl said.

While her mother was making arrangements for their homeward trip, the girl took a particularly bad turn. A doctor was summoned and he said she was dying. Her grief-stricken mother sat by her bedside and the girl's last wish came in a mere whisper.

'Mother, my heart is in Glencairn, please let it rest there.'

After their sad loss, the girl's heartbroken parents left Glencairn and sold it to a family by the name of Bushe. A member of that family held the rank of colonel and was later to fight with the British army in the Crimean War. When the war ended in 1856, Colonel Bushe retired to the family home, which was vacant at the time. He employed staff, but after a few nights in the servants' quarters, they insisted on being given alternative accommodation. Bewildered, he said that there was nowhere else – except over the stables. They willingly agreed to accept this offer and moved their belongings. The Colonel had been used to batmen attending to his every beck and call and soon realised that it was most inconvenient to have to go outside to call a servant if he happened to require something during the night. He begged them to return to their proper quarters in Glencairn House. They still refused. When pressed for a reason, one spoke up.

'Sir, we hears footsteps at night and there do be all sorts of noises coming from the attic.'

Another said, 'And sir, I seen a young lassie dressed all in white and she crying. She were walking down the back stairs from the attic.'

Exasperated by such nonsense, Colonel Bushe dismissed the staff and employed servants from another area. He vowed to forbid them leaving the estate, in case they would hear the silly stories his sacked servants would surely be spreading around the locality.

The new employees duly arrived, but after two nights they too requested alternative accommodation, and gave him the same reasons for wishing to leave the house.

In desperation, Bushe invited an old friend, Seigne, who had an interest in the paranormal, to visit Glencairn House. Seigne was delighted to accept the invitation, and when he arrived, he listened to Bushe's story with enthusiasm. They stayed up late, chatting, and when they retired to bed, it was after midnight.

Bushe awoke some time later and heard light footsteps in the attic above. He was astounded, because he had never heard them before. Then he heard the attic door opening and closing and, after a while, more gentle footsteps coming down the stairs.

When Bushe arrived down for breakfast next morning, his guest was in fine form, rubbing his hands as he sat at the table.

'By Jove, your servants were perfectly correct, there is surely some spirit walking your attic, you lucky fellow,' he said.

The Colonel and Seigne compared notes and it turned out that both had heard similar noises at exactly the same time. They spent the day searching the house, particularly the attic, for something that might hint at an explanation. They found nothing.

Seigne waited a few more days. They heard the noises again and carried out further searches but still the mystery remained. Seigne was apologetic when he had to leave without providing any solution.

A few nights after Seigne's departure, Colonel Bushe was in bed when he heard the footsteps once more. He knew he was alone in the house because the servants had retired to the out-offices hours earlier. Although he had experienced fear on the battlefield, it was nothing to what followed. Previously, the footfalls had gradually faded away, but now they were approaching his bedroom. Closer and closer. A shaft of moonlight lit the doorknob and Bushe saw it turn slowly. Then the door creaked as it opened. A beautiful young girl entered and, smiling, approached the end of his bed. Her right hand was over her heart and she removed it as if in greeting. Through her flimsy clothing, Bushe noticed a wound on her breast.

'Father!' Her voice was the softest and sweetest he had ever heard.

'I am not your father, child,' he managed to stammer.

The girl's smile faded. Her hand flew back to cover the wound and, in an instant, she disappeared. The moon had retreated behind clouds, but Bushe heard his bedroom door opening and closing, light footsteps moving upstairs and then the attic door opening and closing.

Bushe realised that he was perspiring profusely. In fact, his bedclothes were drenched, so he lit a candle, went to the bathroom and dried himself off with a towel. He cursed the missing servants, whom, if closer to hand, he would have aroused to prepare fresh linen for his bed. When he glanced in the mirror he hardly recognised himself, so pale and trembling was his face.

'I will have to solve this mystery tomorrow,' he vowed to his image.

After breakfast he went to the attic and began to examine everything in minute detail. He opened drawers, scrutinised the contents of an old wardrobe and some dusty boxes. By noon there was only one item remaining to be checked – a worn travel trunk that had been there as long as he remembered. He recalled hearing someone say that it had belonged to a previous owner. He was pessimistic about its contents shedding any light on the matter, because Seigne and he had opened it during their search and saw that it contained only useless bric-à-brac. This time, however, he took out each item and examined it closely – a porcelain bull and matador, a worn leather purse embossed with a cockerel, two belts, a scarf, a small pair of gloves and a diary for the year 1795.

Leafing through the diary, Bushe read in faint, dainty handwriting the story of the delicate girl who had lived in Glencairn House and who had gone abroad for the sake of her health. The entries ended on 25 June with the sentence: 'My heart is in Glencairn, please God, let it rest there.' Then he spotted something wrapped in an old Italian newspaper, tied with red ribbon. The paper was yellowed with age and its edges were frayed but Bushe could read the date – 30 June 1795. He placed it on a dressing table and untied the ribbon. There lay a small wooden box with a tiny brass clasp, which the Colonel lifted. A yellow silk bag with a draw cord was inside – a lady's money purse, he thought. But in the bag he found a small sealed metal canister and a piece of parchment with the words: 'This box contains the heart of a young girl who died in Rome, Italy on 29 June 1795. Her dying wish was that it should rest in Glencairn House.'

Astounded, Bushe immediately summoned Seigne, who hurried to Glencairn. Together they opened the canister and found a small, embalmed heart. Seigne read the parchment and the two men began speculating on what might have transpired. Obviously, the girl's mother had gone to enormous trouble to honour her daughter's request and Seigne's experience suggested that the child's spirit should be at rest.

Suddenly he realised what was amiss and he shouted excitedly. 'I have it! The girl had asked that her heart should rest in Glencairn. What she intended was that it should be buried there. Her mother went to the trouble of having it embalmed and sealed but what the girl had craved was its interment in that beautiful woodland surrounding this house – her beloved home.'

The two men selected a spot under an oak tree beside the Blackwater and there they buried the girl's heart. They kept the precise location a secret and revealed it to no one. Thereafter, there were no more footsteps, noises or apparitions in Glencairn House.

TWENTY FOUR

THE MAYO BÉICHEADÁN

A west of Ireland ghost had its own name – Béicheadán, which means 'bawler' or 'yeller', even though it is headless, so we must assume that even without a mouth, a ghost can scream. It inhabited Barnalyra Wood, a fine larch forest south of Charlestown, County Mayo, which covered a vast area until it was cut down after a poor turf-harvest in a nearby bog during 1924. Everyone in the area believed the ghost existed. Parents scared bold children by cruelly warning them that Béicheadán would come and take them away if they didn't behave themselves. When Charles Bianconi's coaches began travelling the Sligo–Galway route, his coachmen knew of the headless ghost and they made sure to be clear of Barnalyra before nightfall. The story originated long before the coaches came, however.

At the end of the seventeenth century, a poor man, his wife and daughter, Eileen, lived in a clearing near the road. The girl grew up to be a beautiful young woman and her parents were perturbed that they could offer no dowry. They knew that without one she would have to be content with marrying some local ne'er-do-well.

A retired sea captain was riding a fine horse from Sligo to Galway one evening. It was getting late and he had good reason to seek lodgings for the night. In his saddlebag he had something worth protecting and he knew that highwaymen often hid in the wood and attacked travellers. He called at the house of the poor people and asked if he could stay the night with them. Fearful of strangers, Eileen ran to her room before he saw her. The man explained that all he required was a good meal and a clean bed for himself, and a stable and some oats for his horse. He promised to reward them well and tapped his bulging saddlebag knowingly. The old couple exchanged glances and although they had no spare room, they welcomed the stranger. While the men were talking by the fire, the *bean a' tí* went to Eileen's room and

they both prepared the bed with fresh linen and dusted down the furniture. Then the girl took her belongings, escaped through the window and crossed the wood to her grandmother's house. Her mother warned her not to come back next day without checking first that there was no horse in the stable.

The woman then began preparing a meal. She overheard the stranger telling her husband how he had made plenty of money during his lifetime at sea and that since he was now retired, he had sold his ship in Sligo for a good price. He had been reared by foster-parents who were now elderly and living in the southern tip of the county. Tomorrow he would reach their house and repay them for all they had done for him.

After a good dinner and further conversation, the Captain said, 'Well, I must be on the road early. I will pay you in advance. Thank you for the meal and goodnight.'

He astonished the couple by slapping a gold sovereign on the table. Then they sat on two *súgán* chairs close to the fire and began whispering together. Before long, the woman went to her daughter's bedroom door and peeped through the keyhole. She came back to her husband in a state of excitement.

'Sure as God, he's in there counting out hundreds of gold sovereigns from his saddlebag.

It would provide Eileen with a dowry that will get her the nobleman she deserves.'

The old man seemed reluctant to agree to what his wife was suggesting, but eventually he sighed and nodded his head.

The woman peeped through the keyhole again and listened intently.

'The light is out and he's snoring like a foghorn,' she said.

Her husband reached into the thatch and took down a cleaver.

They killed their lodger, beheaded him and buried the torso as far into the wood as they could carry it. Then the man took his *sleán* and went into a nearby bog, where he buried the head. He returned home, and while his wife hid the stranger's money, he took the horse from the stable, rode it to Swinford and sold it to a hunting landlord.

After a few months, the couple walked to Claremorris to meet a matchmaker with a view to finding a suitable partner for Eileen. It was dusk before they reached the edge of Barnalyra Wood on their way home. From deep within it they heard a bloodcurdling scream and within seconds saw the headless body of their former guest cross the road in front of them. Blood was dripping from his neck and staining his clothes. A bitterly cold, stormforce wind whipped up suddenly, and the scream turned to a mocking laugh as a tree fell and killed the old man. The woman ran home, terrified.

After her husband's burial, she became silent and morose. Eileen called in wise women and quack doctors but no one could tell what was wrong. When a year had almost passed since her father's death, Eileen was sitting close to the fire with her mother one evening. They sat together as the old couple had done when they plotted the Captain's murder. Suddenly the old woman called 'Sshh!' and ran to the door of her daughter's room. To Eileen's astonishment, her mother began blubbering out the story of what she and her husband had done in order to get a dowry. Eileen went to bed saddened, but her mother went out into the night and began crossing the bog, searching for the place where her husband had buried the head of the Captain. She tumbled into a boghole and was drowned.

The shock of hearing her mother's story, followed by the woman's death, deeply affected Eileen's mind. She became deranged. The beautiful young woman stopped eating and became a frail, wrinkled wreck. Each night she stood at the door of the cabin staring blankly into the wood and then towards the bog. The screams and laughs of Béicheadán seemed to move from the wood to the bog and back again. Constantly. Terrifyingly. Until they tore her sanity apart.

TWENTY FIVE

BLOODY SUNDAY REVISITED?

Until the late Mícheál Ó hAodha's biography of Mícheál Mac Liammóir was published in 1990 it had always been accepted that the actor was born in Blackrock, County Cork, as he had claimed. In fact, he was born in Willesden, London. Affected, ever acting, courteous but occasionally domineering, Mac Liammóir came across as a vain man. Close acquaintances however, testify to his warm and winning personality. He often regaled friends with startling tales, which suggested that he was a person with strong psychic powers.

Once, while playing Oberon in *A Midsummer Night's Dream*, Mac Liammóir received a letter from one Vivian Butler-Burke. A cheque for one hundred pounds was enclosed, as a token of admiration for his performance and for opening the donor's eyes to the 'Gates of Fairyland'. Mac Liammóir accepted an invitation to lunch at the Gresham hotel and met this sixty-year-old admirer, her escort (a small Indian gentleman, who later disappeared) and her dog Connla. She told Mícheál that he hadn't changed a bit!

That was strange, for they had never met, at least according to Mac Liammóir. But Vivian insisted (and she swore that Connla agreed with her) that they had known each other in a previous incarnation, when Mac Liammóir belonged to a different race: Persian or perhaps Chaldean, she claimed. When Mac Liammóir told her he couldn't accept the cheque, she reprimanded him, saying, 'Well, I see you haven't changed. You are as obstinate as ever!' The pair compromised. She would accept shares in the Gate Theatre to the value of one hundred pounds.

Because Mac Liammóir's partner, Hilton Edwards, found Butler-Burke tiresome, he did not accompany Mícheál when he went on some of her archaeological trips and 'sentimental masquerade[s] that cloaked a half forgotten sincerity'. He tolerated her enthusiasm and 'mild paganism', consoling himself that 'only the simple can accompany the great on the eternal cavalcade'. Her part in the evolution of the Gate was 'incongruous, maddening and quite inexplicable'.

At the end of the Gate's 1934 summer season, Vivian had been missing for some months when Mac Liammóir met her walking her dog one morning in St Stephen's Green. She had news for him, she said. He was a Navajo Indian! And it had been revealed to her that he was going to America! America was in the air; did he not feel it?

Mac Liammóir studied her closely in wonder. There was no possible way that she could have known about the telegram in his pocket. It had arrived from Orson Welles in New York before Mac Liammóir had set out for his walk. It invited the Gate company to join him for a summer season at Woodstock, Illinois.

Another story tells how, as a boy actor in London in 1916, a young British army officer befriended Mac Liammóir. The pair made a solemn pact that whoever died first would return to visit the other. The officer lost his life soon after at the Battle of the Somme and, following a period of sadness, Mícheál forgot about him and their agreement.

Around 1936, Mícheál awoke one morning in his Dublin apartment. Only a weak wash of light was coming through the drawn curtains. His bedroom door opened and his friend of twenty years ago stood by his bed, leaving a tray with his morning coffee on the bedside locker.

'You have returned after all these years?' Mícheál asked.

The officer smiled and nodded, then crossed the room to open the curtains. In the full light, Mícheál saw that it was, in fact, his newly engaged manservant.

All imagination? Well, maybe, but when Mac Liammóir became better acquainted with his servant, he discovered that he had been batman to the officer.

After rehearsing late into the night on one occasion, Mac Liammóir returned home with Hilton Edwards to find their house without electricity. Edwards moved upstairs quickly but as Mac Liammóir slowly followed, despite the darkness, he saw a distraught man in British army uniform dashing past him, chased by four others. When he reached their apartment and Edwards told him he had not seen anything, Mac Liammóir was quite overcome.

He made enquiries and learned that the house was one of those raided by the IRA on Bloody Sunday morning, 21 November 1920. A British serviceman was shot there. Mac Liammóir was convinced that he had witnessed the scene re-enacted.

Author's note: (Most accounts of Bloody Sunday's events state that the victims were agents who operated in plain clothes and that many of them were in bed. However, there are also claims that some uniformed officers were disturbed and, in one case, shot.)

TWENTY SIX

A LONGFORD DOG

The County Longford folklorist Pádraig Mac Gréine related a ghost story with a difference, in that the ghost's presence was more or less permanent. Over the years the story has been embellished in the retelling but the gist remains the same.

A man named Sheridan lived on the side of Corn (sometimes Carn) Hill near Drumlish, County Longford. Locals spelt and pronounced the name 'Shurdan'. When he was a boy, one of his close friends died. That boy's ghost began consorting with Shurdan and grew up along with him. The spirit hunted with him and was not afraid of a little work. He guarded Shurdan's crops too – even his turf. The ghost became troublesome, however, when he insisted on socialising with his friend. Most evenings, Shurdan played cards in a neighbour's house. The ghost went along too and other players may have wondered if, perhaps, he could see through their cards and pass on the information to his friend.

One night two women of the household went out to the haggard for turf. The ghost followed them and would not let them fill their baskets. They went back and complained to Shurdan.

Shurdan went out with them and asked the ghost, 'What's this all about?'

'I want you to come home out of this place,' the ghost replied.

'Faith, and I will not,' said Shurdan, 'for I want to play another few hands.'

'I'm telling you to come away home,' the ghost insisted.

The ghost disappeared and Shurdan helped the women fill the baskets and they all returned to the kitchen. Under the table where he had been sitting, Shurdan saw a large black dog that not been there before. The animal was glaring at him with fiery red eyes and green saliva was dripping from its mouth. Shurdan felt his stomach heave with fear. This surely was a pooka, he thought, so bidding the rest of the players farewell, he went home.

Nobody else in the house saw the dog but during the next game of cards two brothers began arguing. A fight broke out. One man reached for a heavy metal candlestick and struck his brother over the head with it, killing him.

The family blamed Shurdan and his ghost for the falling out that led to the tragedy. Word spread and everyone in the neighbourhood began to shun him, and he decided that he would have to get rid of his constant companion.

The ghost knew what Shurdan was planning and he surprised him by saying one day, 'Whatever you do, don't settle me between the froth and the water.'

Shurdan was not too clear on what the ghost meant, so he kept away from all streams and buried the ghost under a bush. For many years afterwards, this was called the Pooka Bush.

GLOSSARY

Anglo-Irish Treaty: An agreement between Ireland and England signed on 6 December 1921 that gave independence to twenty-six counties of Ireland (*see* War of Independence, *below*).

Banshee: Lit. Fairy Woman. (*Bean*, woman *Sidhe*, fairy). A spectre said to wail when death in certain families is imminent.

bean a' tí: Woman of the House

Bloody Sunday: 21 November 1920. Michael Collins' 'Squad' augmented by other Dublin IRA volunteers shot dead fourteen British Secret Service agents in their Dublin homes. Auxiliary forces retaliated by killing Dick McKee, Conor Clune and Peadar Clancy, while Black and Tans opened fire indiscriminately at a Gaelic football match in Croke Park, killing twelve people.

Civil War, Irish: During 1922–23 former comrades in the War of Independence fought each other as a result of acceptance of the Anglo-Irish Treaty (*see above*).

clochán: Beehive-shaped hut of dry masonry with a corbel roof.

cromlech: Circle of upright prehistoric rocks forming a tomb.

Garda Síochána: Lit. Guard of the Peace. Irish police force.

haggard: Area of a farmyard where hay and straw are stored.

IRA: Irish Republican Army

mearing: Boundary ditch or fence separating two farms.

práiscín: An apron made from coarse material.

Saorstát Éireann: The Irish Free State. Twenty-six counties of Ireland freed as a result of the War of Independence (*see below*).

scailtín: Hot whiskey (hot toddy) with additions such as butter, honey or cloves.

sleán: Two winged spade for cutting turf.

súgán: Straw rope

United Irishmen: The Society of United Irishmen, founded in Belfast and in Dublin in October and November 1791 respectively. Originally it sought parliamentary reform but later dedicated itself to the establishment of a republic.

War of Independence: Also known as the Anglo-Irish War. After the 1916 Rebellion in Dublin and the execution of its leaders, hostilities became widespread, leading to Volunteer (IRA, *see above*) action against Crown forces between 21 January 1919 and the Truce of 11 July 1921, which led to the signing of the Anglo-Irish Treaty on 6 December 1921 (*see above*).